MW00896630

Cabby Potts,

DUCHESS OF DIRT

Kathleen Wilford

Blue Bronco Books • New Jersey

To Mom and Dad, with love

First edition 2022.

Our books may be purchased in bulk at a discount for promotional,
educational, and business use.
Please contact The Little Press sales department by email at
info@littlepresspublishing.com
Library of Congress Control Number: 2022937440
ISBN 978-1-956378-04-7 (paperback)
ISBN 978-1-956378-05-4 (hardback)
ISBN 978-1-956378-06-1 (Ebook)

Book design by Harini Rajagopalan
Text by Kathleen Wilford
Edited by Sue Davison and Michele McAvoy
The Little Press
P.O. Box 35, Wood-Ridge, N.J. 07075
www.littlepresspublishing.com

Printed in India

Contents

— *Part 1* —

A Tragic and Ironical Fate

Chapter 1

"Skunk fat. Says right here, it's just the thing for greasing your boots and rubbing on sores." I held up the newest edition of *Prairie Farmer* for my sister Emmeline to see, in case she didn't believe me.

"Fat? From a *skunk*? That's revolting," Emmeline sniffed. "Your taste in literature is so unrefined. Besides, you're supposed to be sorting the mail, not reading it, Cabby." She hefted a heavy canvas *U.S. Mail* sack and turned it upside down. As letters, magazines, and newspapers spilled across the post office floor, she pounced on a ladies magazine.

"Ha! You read people's mail too," I said, "and you're the postmistress." I rolled my eyes as Emmeline turned the magazine pages, no doubt looking for the next installment of some romantic story. "*My* taste in literature is better than . . ."

There was a knock on the post office door. I jumped, hiding the *Prairie Farmer* behind my skirt.

The top half of the door swung open, and my brother Orin's freckly face appeared. "Hey, Em. Hey, Cabby. Guess where Ma and Pa are."

"At the bank, right?" Emmeline said.

"Nope. They're across the street at the Grand Paris Hotel. Drinking *coffee*. With a *stranger*."

"You're making that up," I snorted. I hadn't seen any strangers around, and Ma would never spend a nickel on hotel coffee.

"They want to see you right away, Cabby," Orin finished, folding his arms importantly across his chest. It wasn't often my younger brother got to be the man with the news.

I gulped and turned to Emmeline, but she looked as confused as I was. "What's going on, Orin?" I demanded.

"Dunno. Pa wouldn't say."

I slid the *Prairie Farmer* into Mr. Hanley's slot, stomped past Orin, and hurried through Nehemiah Meacham's General Store and Post Office. I had to thread through a line of folks waiting for my sister to open the post office, which was in a back room of the store. Outside, warm, early-June sunshine flooded Main Street, but I felt a mite shiverish. Was I in trouble?

I crossed the railroad tracks in the middle of the street, then mounted the board sidewalk on the opposite side, my steps dragging. What if the stranger was the postmaster general? Could you go to jail for reading people's magazines?

I took a breath and pushed open the door to the Grand Paris Hotel, my heart thumping hard. Low voices came from the parlor off the hall. I walked into the tiny room with faded rose wallpaper, and the voices stopped. My parents sat in two chairs, both of them as stiff as fence posts. A plump lady in a green dress and black bonnet sat on the sofa, squinting at me like I was a chicken she was sizing up for Sunday dinner.

"My daughter, Catherine Potts," Ma said.

Yipes. My parents called me "Catherine" only on important occasions—or when I was in trouble. Even if it wasn't post office trouble, there were other possibilities. Just last week I had let a bat loose in the house, thinking it would catch the mosquitos. Who knew it would fly into Emmeline's hair?

"Sit down, Catherine," said the lady. "'Ow old are you?"

I sat carefully on the wobbly chair in the corner of the room. After a long moment when the words wouldn't come, I managed to croak, "I'm twelve. And a half."

"Is the girl simple?" the lady said impatiently. She had a funny way of talking, like she had marbles in her mouth, and she didn't seem fond of the letter *h*. She wasn't from Kansas, that was for sure. She also didn't look like a postmaster general, although you never knew. Her dress had braided trim on the sleeves and under the folds of her double chin. It made Ma's go-to-town calico seem shabby.

"My daughter is not simple, Mrs. Shaw," Ma said. She leaned forward in her chair, tense as a fiddle string, an untouched cup of coffee in her lap. Pa looked down, picking at a thread on his trousers with dirt-lined finger-nails.

"Catherine is clever enough," Ma went on. "And she is industrious and obedient."

I blinked, befuddled. Usually, Ma said I was hasty, or reckless, or had a big mouth—an "intemperate tongue" was how she put it.

"Good," said Mrs. Shaw. "'Er Ladyship won't abide a

lazy girl." She wagged a stubby finger at me. "You understand?"

I *didn't* understand. "Ladyship?" was all I could think to say. This was a person, not a boat, apparently.

"Lady Ashford, of course," Mrs. Shaw said. "Just arrived from London. She wants an 'ardworking girl, and quiet and clean and cheerful."

Wants a girl? Quiet and clean?

"Your mother says you can lay a table proper, and do washing and mending and such. Is that right?"

No! I wanted to say. *Whatever you're talking about, you have the wrong person. I help my pa in the fields and look after the cow and tote the water. I help my sister in the post office, sometimes. I am nobody's "girl"!*

Ma was glaring at me, so what I actually said was, "Yes, Ma'am." It was true I could set the table and do the wash, although mending was my weak point, to put it mildly. But all that was indoor work, and I was an outdoor kind of girl.

"There's to be no uproar in the 'ouse, nor backtalk," Mrs. Shaw continued. "'Er Ladyship won't 'ave it."

"No, Ma'am," I said automatically, although I was only half listening. My brain buzzed like it was full of gnats.

As Mrs. Shaw and Ma kept talking, I turned to my father. "What's going on, Pa?" I whispered.

Pa rubbed a hand through his messy, sandy-colored hair, something he did when he was confused or bothered about something. "Well, Cabby, Mrs. Shaw here is housekeeper for the Honest Nigel Ashford, as I think he is called."

Mrs. Shaw stopped talking and frowned at Pa like he'd spit on the floor. "*Honorable.* The *Honorable* Nigel

Ashford is 'is name."

"Oh, right," Pa said. "We met Mrs. Shaw at the bank, and she was pinning up this advertisement, you see. Your Ma . . . we . . . well, we thought of you." He handed me a piece of paper, and I forced my eyes to focus on the words.

Housemaid Wanted

Steady, respectable girl required
for housework and cleaning
Home of the Honorable Nigel Saint-James Ashford
Ashford Manor, Prince Albert, Kansas
Liberal wages, room and board

Housemaid? What a horrible word! Not that I had ever actually seen a housemaid, but I could picture one: a meek, aproned, pale-faced girl who never saw the sun.

"You want *me*? To . . .?" I touched the paper—the letters seemed icy cold—and Pa nodded.

"What about Emmeline? Why can't she do it?" I blurted, although I knew it was an awful thing to say.

"Cabby!" Ma snapped.

"Your sister has a job," Pa said patiently. "And you're too young to be postmistress."

It felt as if a piano had landed on my shoulders. "Would I have to go every day?"

Ma and Pa glanced at each other. Pa rubbed at his hair. Then he put out a finger, tapping one of the lines. *Liberal wages, room and board . . .*

The words snaked off the page, wrapped themselves

around my throat, and cut off the air. "Room and . . . You want me to *live* there?"

"Well, naturally," Mrs. Shaw said, drawing her eyebrows together.

"Wh-where is Prince Albert? Is it far?" I had heard of the new town of Prince Albert—a "community of culture and refinement," according to the newspaper—but I had no idea where it was.

"Not far," Pa said. He put his hand on my knee but didn't look at me. "Down the railroad line maybe twelve miles from Slocum City . . . or fifteen, from our place."

Fifteen miles!

I pulled away from Pa's hand and jumped to my feet. I would refuse. They couldn't make me do this. I took a deep, shaky breath and opened my mouth. But before I could say anything, Ma stabbed me with the *look*. "Go on outside, Cabby. We have things to discuss with Mrs. Shaw."

There was no arguing with the *look*. It seemed there was no arguing with Ma at all.

For some unimaginable reason, my mother and father wanted to send me away.

Chapter 2

I stumbled down the hall, hurrying past Adelaide Buchanan, her arms full of laundered sheets, her eyes and mouth perfect *o*'s of curiosity. I liked Adelaide, even if she was a town girl, but I was in no mood for questions.

Outside the hotel, I collapsed onto a bench. Amazingly, Slocum City looked perfectly normal: horses swishing their tails at the hitching rail; Mrs. Snopes, the barber's wife, emptying a pan of water into the road; my brothers Orin and Jesse throwing a ball to each other farther down the street. The wind blew hard like it always did, making the canvas awning over my head snap and creak.

I stared at the advertisement in my hand. Why would Ma and Pa make me do this? I knew times were hard. We didn't even have two dollars a year for a magazine subscription, at least according to Ma. But weren't we just temporarily inconvenienced? That was what Pa always said when we couldn't buy something: "Can't get that today, my dears. We're temporarily inconvenienced."

But Pa was never too upset about our lack of money. It had to be Ma's idea, not his, to send me away.

But why?

I did burn the cornbread and make a mess of the

embroidery from time to time. Pretty regularly, to tell the truth. Maybe she was sending me away to make me *domestic.*

But I could milk our cow without spilling a drop; I could find her when she lay down in the grass with only her horns sticking up. I could hoe the cornfield for hours on end, harness the horses and carry their feed, and swing a sickle without decapitating anyone. I was a useful daughter, at least outside the house.

I crumpled the paper and mashed it into a ball. Take that, Ashford Manor! I chucked the balled-up paper onto the board sidewalk . . . and bounced it off a shiny, pointy-toe boot. The boot was topped by brown trousers with perfect creases, an orange waistcoat with a watch chain disappearing into the pocket, and a pale, handsome face with a turned-up moustache. My second stranger of the day, even more high-falutin' than Mrs. Shaw. I pegged him at twenty-two, or thereabouts.

"Sorry, mister." I grabbed the crumpled ball of paper and sat down on the bench, tucking my feet under my skirt.

The stranger gave me a narrow-eyed glance. Then he straightened his spotless, already-straight shirt cuffs and looked out across Main Street. The buildings were mostly just false-front board shacks—even the Grand Paris Hotel, although it did have a genuine second floor. Some of the buildings were empty now, with the prairie grass smack against their walls. But it was my town, and I hoped he wasn't thinking bad things about it.

All at once the stranger stood up taller. "*That* is an uncommonly pretty girl," he said low, talking to himself.

My heavens, he was looking straight at Emmeline. She

was coming our way, hurrying across the railroad tracks.

It was true—my sister *was* uncommonly pretty, even in her faded, let-down dress and floppy sunbonnet. She had glossy hair the color of chestnuts, big brown eyes, and a dimple that popped in and out of her cheek. But the way the stranger said it, it was like spotting a pretty girl in Slocum City was a mighty rare event, like finding a lump of gold in the dirt of the street. This struck me as a superior attitude.

"*That* is my sister, Miss Emmeline Potts," I said. Good thing Ma couldn't hear me being so forward.

The stranger looked at me more closely. His eyebrows lifted. I knew what he was thinking: I didn't look at all like my seventeen-year-old sister. Pa said I was as pretty as a Kansas sunflower, but a sunflower was basically a weed. I had messy hair the color of cornstalks and no figure whatsoever, which I considered a good thing, since girls with figures had to wear corsets to nip in their waists.

Before the stranger could say anything, Emmeline rushed up, staring from me to him instead of looking where she was going. Wouldn't you know it, she tripped over the toe of a busted-up shoe and caught the other foot in the hem of her dress. She was about to dive into the dirt when the stranger sprang off the sidewalk and grabbed her by the arm.

"Oh!" she squeaked, wobbling upright and blushing pink. "Thank you!"

"My pleasure," said the gentleman, letting go of her arm and making a little bow. "A very good morning, Miss . . . Pitts, is it?"

"Yes, no . . . I mean, it's Potts. I'm Emmeline."

I almost laughed. My sister was so consternated by male attention she couldn't recall her own name. Then I remembered the advertisement balled in my hand and the awful thing that had just happened to me.

"Em," I said. "Can we go?"

"Isn't it a lovely day?" the gentleman said, ignoring me. "Doesn't this fresh breeze simply stir the senses?"

Emmeline blushed even deeper. It was safe to say she had never heard the Kansas wind described in this exact way. "Yes, yes it does," she said faintly. "The breeze is so *very* fresh."

I couldn't stand it. I hopped off the sidewalk and took my sister by the elbow. "Nice to meet you, mister, but we have to get going."

"Cabby!" Emmeline whispered furiously.

"But I haven't introduced myself," the gentleman said, giving yet another bow. "I am the Honorable Nigel Cedrick Saint-James Ashford."

Good gracious, this was Nigel Ashford of Ashford Manor. I suddenly felt sick. My parents wanted me to work for *him*?

"My father," he said, "is Lord Edward Bickford-Smythe Ashford, eighteenth Earl of Tewking-hamshire—in England, of course."

"Oh my!" Emmeline breathed, but I felt like screaming. Who cares who this high-and-mighty Englishman's father is? *My father,* I wanted to say, *is Albert E. Potts, first Prince of the Prairie—in Kansas, of course.* Maybe if I was sassy enough, I'd be fired before my job even started.

But I couldn't do it. Potts girls were not rude to strangers in the middle of Main Street. I stood there, my fists clenched.

"Until we meet again," the gentleman said. He nodded to me and leaned over and took my sister's hand in his slim, white fingers. Then he kissed her hand—right there for anyone to see—before stepping onto the sidewalk and strutting away, his shoes tap-tapping on the crooked boards.

Emmeline stared after him in a daze, holding out the hand he had kissed like it was paralyzed or something. I stared after him too, stunned. Then, out of nowhere, the tears flooded my eyes. I started to bawl.

Chapter 3

"Heavens, Cabby, what's the matter?" Emmeline said, snapping out of her daze. "Are you sick? Is somebody dead? Is that why Ma and Pa wanted you?"

"N-n-no," I hiccupped. I wasn't the crying type, normally, but when I got going, I was a shuddering mess.

"Come on." Emmeline led the way across the street, through the dark, stuffed-with-stuff general store, and back into the post office. She closed the door and put her arms around me. She was the nicest sister you could ask for, even if lately her brain was addled with romance and refinement.

"Em, Ma and Pa want to send me away!" I sobbed.

"What? No, they don't."

"*Ma* does." I pushed the wadded-up paper into her hands.

Emmeline started to unfold the paper, but just then there was a knock at the door. The top half opened, and a white cat jumped onto the ledge, hissing at us.

"S-s-stop that, M-M-Moonbeam," said a voice, and a huge hand pushed the cat off the ledge. The proprietor of the store, Nehemiah Meacham—Knee-High, as folks called him, ironically—leaned in, his big head and shoulders filling the space. "I . . . are you t-t-two all right?" He looked at me then at Emmeline, turning almost as red as the whiskers on his face.

Knee-High, if not his nasty cat, was a friend. I looked forward to Tuesdays and Fridays, post office days, partly to talk to him. But I wasn't ready to tell him what had happened. "We're all right," I sniffed, wiping my face with my sleeve.

Emmeline dimpled at Knee-High. "Thank you for asking, though." I could tell she was in a hurry to get rid of him. As soon as he had shut the door, she laid the paper on a stool and smoothed it with her hand. Her eyes got wide. "What is this?"

"See? Ma and Pa want me to be a housemaid at Ashford Manor . . ."

"*Ashford*? Nigel Ashford? He lives in a *manor*?"

"Did you hear what I said? Ma and Pa are making me . . ."

"He's *nobility*," Emmeline breathed. "Son of a real live English Lord. And he kissed my hand, just like in 'Fair Lillian.'"

"Emmeline! This is real life, not *stories*."

She tossed the paper down and hugged me. "I'm sorry. Is it really true? Do you have to go away?"

Just then the door opened again—no knock this time—and Ma appeared, Orin and Jesse beside her. "I expected you to wait outside, Cabby," she snapped. "Emmeline, have you finished your work?"

"No, Ma, I was just . . ."

Ma pushed the boys inside. "Keep Orin and Jesse with you, and finish up quickly. Cabby, you come with me."

The events of the next few hours—more discussions with Mrs. Shaw, a stormy ride home in the wagon, a miserable supper—are too tragic to describe. My tears and arguments did nothing to change Ma's mind. My only hope, I figured, was to work on Pa's tender heart when I could get him alone—not an easy task when you live in a one-room house made of squares of prairie sod.

Finally, after the supper dishes were wiped, Ma headed to the outhouse, or the "necessary," as Emmeline called it, thinking the term more refined. Pa sat at the table, fiddling dejectedly with an unlit pipe. I hurried to face him across the table. "Please, Pa, don't make me do this!" Tears ran down my cheeks, and my heart felt as squeezed as a wrung-out rag.

Orin and Jesse put their arms around my waist. "We don't want Cabby to go away," Jesse wailed. He was only six, and Orin was ten.

"Please, Pa," Emmeline said, her voice quivering, "don't tear Cabby from the bosom of her family."

Seeing his beloved offspring in tears should have been enough to win Pa over. Right then he should have said, "Don't worry, chickees, things will work out. I'm sure Ashford Manor can find itself a different house-maid."

Pa was always sure things would work out. When something *didn't* work out, he was sure the next thing *would,* which explains why we moved around so much before Kansas.

But Pa only looked down at the table and rubbed his hair until it stood on end. "Cabby's to be paid two dollars a week," he mumbled.

Orin stopped sniffling. "Two dollars a week? We'll be rich!"

There was a loyal brother for you.

Pa shook his head, glancing at Ma as she came back in. "No, we won't be rich, exactly. You see, we're uh . . . powerfully inconvenienced at the moment."

"*I* know that— " I began.

"Listen, children," Ma said. She leaned into Pa's chair, so that she and Pa faced all of us across the table. I noticed how threadbare the sleeves of her dress were. You could practically see through them. "Maybe you don't understand," Ma said. "Even with a good harvest this year, we won't make enough to get through the winter. We're hanging on by our fingernails here."

"Ma's right," Pa said. "We need the money. Or else . . ."

"Or else what?" Orin squeaked.

Ma and Pa looked at each other, and, with a sinking heart, I knew or else what.

A family of homesteaders nearby had relinquished their claim this spring. They put up a sign we used to pass on our way to town:

Eaten by Grasshoppers

Kansas, 1875

In Slocum City, Mr. and Mrs. Prouty had given up the boarding house they owned. Mr. Prouty pinned a notice on the door:

In God I trusted—
In Kansas I busted

"Or else" meant give up on our claim—and that would rip the heart right out of me.

"If we did have to give up the claim," Pa said, like he was reading my mind, "I'm sure something else would turn up."

I felt my blood go cold, remembering all the times Pa had said that before. He said it in South Bend, Indiana and Cleveland, Ohio, and a little place in Pennsylvania called Slippery Rock. But I thought he was done saying it now. I thought we were *home.*

"I saw an advertisement in the paper. There's a new kind of stove pipe everyone wants. Corrugated, or something like that," Pa said almost cheerfully. "We could go to Kansas City, sell stove pipes to all the folks going west."

"But Pa," Emmeline said, "we've moved so much already . . ."

Pa said something back, but I stopped listening. I barely remembered Slippery Rock, only how Pa was going to make a lot of money from a salt well—before the explosion, that is. I did remember Cleveland, how we had lived all crammed together in one room of a boarding house while Pa and a Mr. Black made plans to sell Black's Special Elixir, which was going to cure every malady known to mankind. I never knew exactly what happened, but Mr. Black ended up leaving town suddenly, with all Pa's money. After Cleveland, Pa had worked for a while at that awful ironworks in South Bend, while we stayed with Uncle Jed and Aunt Tildy—six long months of Ma hushing us and saying we should be grateful for charity from relatives.

I didn't remember Ma smiling once while we lived in South Bend. Not until Pa brought home a brochure with a horse and a plow on the cover, a lazy river and miles of green fields beyond them. *The State of Kansas*, the title said, *Great Inducements Offered to Homesteaders.*

I remembered how Pa whistled with amazement: all you had to do was file a claim for fourteen dollars, then build a house and make improvements, like growing crops, on the land. After five years and four more dollars, the homestead would belong to you. A quarter-section of government land, one hundred and sixty acres, would belong to *us,* the first land we'd ever owned. The first real home we'd ever had.

"A deal at twice the price," Pa had said.

Now that I thought about it, he hadn't said it much lately.

Not since the grasshoppers.

Chapter 4

I got up from the table and stumbled out the door, almost tripping over our dog, Snuff. "Sorry, pup," I said, and he licked my hand.

To the west, the sky was spread out like a painting, with bands of orange and red and dark blue. I remembered a sunset just like this one, after Pa had finished building our sod house. All six of us stood in the open doorway, looking out at the sky. "Just remember," Ma said, "our house is small, but the land is big."

"Why, Martha," Pa teased, "are you getting sentimental?"

"Nonsense," Ma said, but I heard the happiness in her voice.

That was three years ago. Our claim was nothing but raw prairie then, but it wasn't hard to imagine row upon row of cornstalks, acre upon acre, as far as you could see.

I hurried through the thick, wet grass, Snuff at my heels. In the cornfield, the stalks were knee high, with stiff, strong leaves, ten on each stalk. I knew how many because I kept track of our corn, watched over it like a proud mama. Hardly any sunflowers were growing among the stalks, thanks to me.

But the corn had been strong and stiff last year too, twenty acres of it.

The grasshoppers had arrived in August, when the corn was shoulder high, the ears already formed. The creatures came in a huge buzzing cloud, dropping out of the sky like living hail, piling on top of each other in squirming heaps. As soon as they fell, they started to eat. They coated every leaf of every plant. You could *hear* them chewing.

We tried setting smoky fires, tried beating them away with sticks. It was no use. By the end of the first day, there was nothing left of the corn but some bare stubs. The cabbage, onions, and pumpkins from our kitchen garden were eaten too. There was nothing we could do.

The next day, they invaded our house. We tried stuffing blankets in the cracks, but they chewed through the cloth, wormed through the sod squares, and dropped from the roof. We swept them out, stepped on them, beat at them, but still they devoured all the cornmeal, ate holes in the quilts, attacked the clothes we were wearing, chewed up our few books. It was enough to drive a person insane.

When they finally left, flying off in great whirring bunches, our claim was picked clean.

The grasshoppers had eaten their way across Kansas, and it was bad for everybody. People from the East sent charity—grasshopper barrels, they were called—and no one was too proud to take things. All our shoes had come from the barrels.

But you can't eat shoes, and it had been a hungry winter.

This spring, we had managed to plant eight acres. But the north field wasn't even plowed. Pa worked at it, but he couldn't afford to hire help. It was like we ran and ran but never went anywhere but backwards.

The logic of the arithmetic closed around me like a trap. To help us keep the homestead, I would have to leave it, go off and earn my two dollars a week. A tragic and ironical fate, as Emmeline would put it.

I heard a rustle near my bare feet, and Snuff barked a warning. I hurried back inside, since dying from a snake-bite would be an even worse fate.

Just barely.

That night, I couldn't sleep. I lay there, listening to everybody breathing. Ma and Pa slept on the other side of a curtain wall from Emmeline and me, with the boys next to them in the trundle bed.

Where would I sleep at Ashford Manor? How could I sleep without my sister beside me? I stared into the dark rafters, my eyes dry and burning.

Long past the time when I thought everyone was asleep, I heard Emmeline whisper, "Cabby, are you awake? I'm going to miss you so much."

"M-me too," I quavered.

"You've got to tell me everything." ·

"About what?"

"You know, Mrs. Shay—"

"Shaw."

"Mrs. *Shaw* and what she said at the hotel . . . Was *he* there?"

Well, my sister had gotten over her sorrow quickly. "No, *he* wasn't there. And Mrs. Shaw didn't say much, just how I need to be quiet and respectable and do mending all the time."

"Oh dear. Poor Cabby." Emmeline turned toward me with a rustle of mattress straw. "Um, anything else?"

"Well, there's a Ladyship." I had almost forgotten that part. "She's coming, or maybe she's already—"

Emmeline sat straight up in bed. "What 'Ladyship'?"

"Shh!"

"Is she his *wife*?"

"Yes . . . I guess she's his wife," I said. I had no idea if this was true, but I was tired of my sister swooning over Nigel Ashford. Maybe this would put an end to it.

Emmeline sank back down in the bed. There was a long silence, then a sniff. "I'm never getting married! I'm going to die an old maid." She sniffed again.

"What are you talking about? You didn't think Mr. Ashford was going to *marry* you, did you?"

"No . . ." she said, although it sounded like "yes." My sister was even crazier than I thought.

"Listen," I said, "there's lots of other people you could marry, if you really wanted to. Personally, I don't understand the rush." I wasn't against marriage as a general idea, but I didn't want Emmeline to leave us. As for me, I wouldn't bother with marrying, at least not right away. I had another plan up my sleeve. As soon as I turned twenty-one, I would file a claim for myself, maybe right next to Pa's. Believe it or not, a woman could do that in Kansas, if she wasn't married.

"Like who? Who could I marry?" Emmeline said.

"Well, there's Bub Skyler." Bub had already proven up on his claim and had a good-sized herd of cows, which made him an eligible bachelor, in my opinion.

"I would never marry Bub Skyler! He has no . . . poetry

about him!"

She was right about that. Bub tended to spit in public, and he didn't smell too good, if you want to know the truth. He lived in a dugout house that was practically a cave, down by a creek.

"Hey!" I said, propping myself on an elbow. "What about Mr. Meacham? He's a nice man, and he lives right in town."

"*Knee-High?*"

"I know he stutters, but there are cures. I saw one advertised in the back of *Harper's*. 'Patented and guaranteed to stop stammering.'"

"You are such a cabbage-head," Emmeline said. "Knee-High Meacham is never going to marry. Plus, he's old! He must be *thirty!*" She giggled.

I giggled too. Somehow it *was* a funny idea, Em and Mr. Meacham. Pretty soon we were both shaking with laughter, holding our hands over our mouths to keep quiet. Just for a while it was like it used to be, sisters and best friends laughing together. For a few minutes, I felt happy.

Chapter 5

Next morning, I hurried out of bed when I heard Pa drop into a chair to pull on his boots. Maybe a miracle had occurred. Maybe he'd say, "There you are, daughter. We've made a terrible mistake . . ." But Pa just headed out the door like he always did. I dragged myself into my clothes and started for the door myself. Maybe sharing my sorrows with our cow, Lissie, would make me feel better.

"Wait a minute, Cabby," Ma called before I could get outside. "I want Orin to milk the cow and water the animals this morning."

"But, Ma . . ."

"I want *you* to iron your dresses. Use plenty of starch and be careful with the collars."

I skulked back into the house. What was the point of ironing anyway? Who cared about a few wrinkles? I didn't say this out loud, of course, but I might have made a face, and I'll admit I slammed the flatiron onto the hot stove.

Ma grabbed me by the shoulders and shook me. "Listen here, young lady, are you going to behave like this at Ashford Manor?"

"No, Ma," I whispered, tears stinging my eyes. I spread a dress on the table, feeling like everything and everyone in the universe was mean and unfair, especially Ma. A wicked part of me hoped Lissie would kick over the bucket when Orin tried to milk her. Milking was *my* job.

Used to be my job.

Two days later, early in the morning, I stood on the sidewalk in front of Nehemiah Meacham's General Store and Post Office wearing my best calico dress, the one with the flowered print and puffed sleeves—and the tiniest scorch mark from my ironing. My hair was braided and pinned up neatly around my head, and Ma's old carpet bag and busted-up valise sat at my feet. I felt like I was going to my own funeral.

"My poor Cabby," Emmeline said, clutching my hand. Pa had dropped the two of us off while he and Ma and the boys took care of the wagon. "This is a *truly* doleful day." She had been more sympathetic since she learned about the Ladyship, I have to say. Not one word about Nigel Ashford.

Just then Mrs. Lucretia Snopes popped out of her husband's Barber Shop and Shave Palace and scuttled over to us. "Going to work for that Lord Ashford, are you, Cabby?" Mrs. Snopes was the busiest busybody in Slocum City and probably the entire state of Kansas.

I nodded miserably.

Mrs. Snopes was only about five feet tall, with sharp little eyes, grayish skin, and gray hair pulled back tight. But every inch of her quivered when gossip was in the air. She tapped my sister on the arm, the scraggly stuffed bird on her hat quaking like mad. "I thought the gentleman was more interested in *you,* Emmeline Potts. I saw how he fawned over you, right in the middle of Main Street."

Emmeline shrank from Mrs. Snopes like that awful bird might actually peck her. Fortunately, Ma and Pa and the boys showed up then, and other people started to gather too. My new job seemed to fascinate everyone in town. Except me.

"The English gent, is he an actual Lord?" somebody asked.

"No, no," Mrs. Buchanan said. The Buchanans ran the Grand Paris Hotel. They were from Ohio, not France, but maybe Grand Ohio Hotel didn't sound fancy enough. "I saw the advertisement," Mrs. Buchanan went on. "He's some kind of 'Honorable.'"

"Nigel Ashford is the fifth son of a Lord," said a man with a black bow tie, neatly trimmed sideburns, and shiny black hair—dyed, according to Emmeline. "Consequently his title is 'Honorable,' but he is to be addressed as *Mister* Ashford." The man was Mr. H. H. Mortimer, local land agent and Slocum City's expert on pretty much everything, even though he'd only been here for a year. Ma didn't like him—she said he was "oily," whatever that meant—but everybody else took his words like gospel.

"Hey, Mr. Mortimer, is it true he's got a gold-plated bathtub?" asked Bub Skyler. Bub wore muddy overalls and held a letter between two potato-shaped fingers—trying not to get it dirty, I reckoned. Bub got a lot of letters, which kind of surprised me.

"Wouldn't hurt you to borrow that bathtub, Bub," someone said, and everyone laughed, including Bub. He was pretty good-natured, even if there was no poetry about him. I didn't laugh, though. The collar of my good dress was too tight, and the hairpins gave me a headache.

"I have paid a visit to Ashford Manor," Mr. H. H. Mortimer said. "I can't speak to the bathtubs, but the abode is furnished with the utmost taste and refinement." Mr. Mortimer always talked like he was giving a speech. *He* never got any letters, though, which was also surprising.

"How fortunate we are," Mr. H. H. Mortimer went on, "to have members of the English nobility in our vicinity."

"They won't last," said Knee-High Meacham suddenly, his head sticking up above the crowd. "Anyway that Ashford f-f-fellow won't. He's nothing but a re . . . re-mitt-mitt . . ." Knee-High seemed to realize how many eyes were on him, and he turned bright red. "Re . . . mittance man!" he said, sounding like he was strangling.

"What's a remittance man?" someone asked. But Knee-High just shook his head and pushed his way to where I stood arm in arm with Emmeline. He handed me a paper sack that looked tiny in his big hand. "For when you m-miss your sister," he said with a shy glance at her. He had deep-set brown eyes, and up close I could tell he was younger than he looked—surely not *thirty*.

I peeked inside the sack. It held two sheets of Knee-High's finest writing paper, two envelopes, and two three-cent stamps. I gulped. What a sad thing, having to write to your own sister like some far-away relation. "Thanks, Mr. Meacham," I whispered.

Mrs. Buchanan touched my arm. "How long are you staying there, Cabby?"

"I—I don't know." It was the question I'd been afraid to ask.

"We'll see," Ma said crisply. "Six months, perhaps, to

start."

Six months? Half a *year*? To *start*? I opened my mouth, but I was too stunned to get any words out.

"At least she won't miss school," Bub said, and people laughed again, since Slocum City didn't have a school or a schoolteacher. No one commented on the practically endless sentence I had just been given. Not even Emmeline. Instead, she squeezed my arm as a light, two-wheeled buggy rolled up the street from the east. The buggy was pulled by a gleaming bay horse and driven by a young man, or maybe a boy.

"Is it *him*? Is it Nigel?" she breathed in my ear. She had stopped talking about Nigel Ashford, but apparently she hadn't stopped thinking about him.

"Huh? I don't know." *Six months . . . six months . . . six months* echoed in my head.

"Whoa, whoa!" shouted the driver, who was *not* Nigel, I saw now. The horse, a mare, didn't listen. She charged right past the store. With some difficulty, the driver turned the buggy around, stopped the mare, and hopped down. He was a boy about my age or a little older, with brown skin and straight dark hair. He looked kind of elegant, I have to say, in buckled knee britches, shiny black boots, and a white waistcoat.

Mrs. Snopes pushed her way out to the street. "You're that *Lewis* boy," she said to the boy, pronouncing "Lewis" like it was a bad word. "What are you doing here?"

Eli Lewis, that's who it was. No wonder I hadn't recognized him. The few times I'd seen Eli before, he wore faded overalls made from a chicken-feed sack. His hair hung over his eyes like he wanted to hide from folks.

Eli's pa ran the livery stable outside of town . . . or maybe his ma. I vaguely remembered hearing that Mr. Lewis had died a while back.

Eli took the mare by the reins. "I'm a groom for Mr. Ashford," he said proudly.

"Oh," said Mrs. Snopes. "Well." I guessed she didn't know what a groom was. Neither did I.

"He cleans up pretty good," said someone in the crowd. "I mean . . . considering."

A bunch of people snickered at that remark, and something stiffened in Eli's face, like a shutter banging closed. He scanned the crowd until he found my face. He knew who I was, it seemed. "Can I take your trunk?" he said coldly. "Mrs. Shaw said to strap it on the back."

Now it was my turn to go stiff. Was he making fun of me? It was obvious I wasn't some kind of grand lady who needed a trunk to hold her pile of clothes. I picked up my bags and held them tight, not answering him.

Emmeline started crying and threw her arms around me. Pa gave me a hug, and the boys did too. Ma squeezed my shoulder quickly, her version of a hug. "Go on, Cabby," she said.

I gripped the handles of the bags so hard my fingernails bit into my palms. "Go *on,* Cabby," Ma repeated. Somehow, my legs started to move. I climbed onto the plush seat of the buggy, stuffing the bags under my feet.

Eli climbed up beside me and shook the reins. We started off, my eyes burning and my throat so tight I couldn't even say goodbye.

Chapter 6

As the buggy rolled down Main Street, the cool wind tugged at my hair and my skirt. Overhead, the blue sky arched like an endless, upside-down bowl. It was a beautiful June day.

Six months from now, snow could be falling. It would be December, only weeks from Christmas. I pushed the thought out of my mind, twisting my fingers together and blinking the tears away. What was the use of crying now? Besides, I was not going to cry in front of Eli Lewis. He was a stranger, not to mention a *boy*.

By the time I had more or less pulled my sorry self together, Eli was slowing the mare in front of a stable a little ways outside town. It was a sagging building made of crooked, grayish boards, *Lewis Livery: Fine Horses and Mules for Sale and Hire* painted on the roof in faded letters. Weather-beaten was the right word for this place. In a fight, the weather had definitely won.

A woman stood in the dusty corral, brushing a spotted pony. She wore a fringed robe and soft moccasins; her black hair hung loose down her back.

"*Kehimi!*" she called when she saw us. "And you are Miss Potts?"

I stared at her. I couldn't help it. This was Mrs. Lewis,

Eli's mother. I had seen her before, of course, at Knee-High's store, and I supposed I knew she was an Indian, or at least the only brown-skinned woman in town. But those times she wore a dress and bonnet like the other ladies.

Finally, I remembered my manners. "Yes, I'm Cabby Potts. Nice to meet you." I wished I hadn't stared, but it was too late now.

"And the mare?" Mrs. Lewis said. "What is her name?" Mrs. Lewis's accent was thick, but I could understand her words.

"Georgiana," Eli mumbled, like the name embarrassed him, and Mrs. Lewis laughed. It *was* a fancy name for a Kansas horse, though Emmeline would have called it refined.

Mrs. Lewis pointed at the horse and said something to Eli in her own language. Her speech sounded strange to me, with clicks and stops in the middle of words, and lots of *g*'s and *k*'s. Still, I could tell Mrs. Lewis was giving Eli one of those don't-forget-such-and-such lectures, the same kind my ma gave me.

"Yes, Ma," Eli said when she was done.

Mrs. Lewis frowned. "*Kehimi . . .*"

Eli glanced at me and shifted in his seat. "Yes, *kgou-gkoy*," he corrected himself. He shook Georgiana's reins, and off we went.

As Eli drove, the silence between us seemed to stretch, quiver, and twang. When I couldn't stand it any longer, I cleared my throat. "Your ma is . . ."

Before I could say "nice"—and I did think Mrs. Lewis

was nice—Eli turned to me with a scowl. "She's *Kiowa*. Not 'Indian.' *Kiowa*." He said the word like "Iowa," only with a *k* in front.

"Oh," I said. There were nosy questions I might have asked, like how a Kiowa woman had come to marry a white man, but that scowl put me off. "Do her . . . do the Kiowa people live around here?" I ventured to say.

Eli's scowl deepened. "Nope."

What a dumb question. Of course the Kiowa people didn't live around here. I remembered a morning at Aunt Tildy and Uncle Jed's house in Indiana. Pa was reading a newspaper article out loud, something about how the tribes had been forced out of Kansas and into Indian Territory to the south.

"Well, that's a blessing," Aunt Tildy said. "One less thing to worry about in Kansas." Aunt Tildy thought homesteading was just another one of Pa's "foolish ventures" and that Kansas was a wild place "simply crawling with Indians."

"I expect it wasn't a blessing for the tribes, being pushed off their land," Pa had said mildly. He tried not to argue with Aunt Tildy.

I glanced sideways at Eli, trying to think of a not-dumb question, which turned out to be difficult. Aside from Eli and his ma, I had been around Indians only once, when Pa took me with him to a camp down toward Indian Territory, where he bought a warm buffalo robe. He had smiled and tried to talk to the people there, but I hung back shyly, not understanding their language. I wondered now if they'd been Kiowa.

"Well, I hope your ma . . . has a nice day," I said. Which

was just about the dumbest comment possible.

Eli didn't answer, but I thought I saw his mouth twitch. Laughing at me, I bet.

We were out on the open prairie now, grass rolling away on both sides like waves of the ocean. The road was just two lines through the grass, which was still bright green and juicy-looking this time of year. Red-winged blackbirds clung to the tall stalks, calling "cock-*lee*, cock-*lee*." A hawk circled overhead, wings dipping on invisible currents of air.

I had hardly ever been this far out on the prairie, and ordinarily I would have enjoyed it. But every turn of the buggy wheel was taking me farther from my home. I slumped in the seat, trying not to think about Ashford Manor and what my new life would be like. If I didn't think about it, I could pretend it wasn't real.

But soon a whistle blew and a train roared past us, steam pouring from the chuffing engine. The 9:05, probably. It was going to the same place I was going, and, unlike me, in an awful hurry to get there. Some people leaned out of the windows and waved to us. I didn't wave back, figuring Eli would laugh at that too.

Soon after the train passed, we came to a place where a long-ago flood had washed out part of the road, making a big dip in the path. "Whoa, Georgiana! Slow down!" Eli ordered, pulling back on the reins. But the mare, who seemed to be an opinionated animal, trotted on. The buggy rolled into the hollow, tipped a little, then lurched wildly. I grabbed for a handle, ended up grabbing at air— and tumbled out of the buggy, landing on my backside in the dirt. Ow!

I scrambled up, brushing dirt off my dress as best I could. My backside throbbed like the dickens. The buggy lay on its side, one wheel spinning. Georgiana stood switching her tail like nothing had happened.

"Help me stand it up, Cabby!" Eli called, panic in his voice. Not "sorry I dumped you in the dirt," mind you, just "help me stand it up."

I stomped over and helped Eli wrestle the buggy upright. "Nothing broken," he panted. "Mr. Ashford would have fired me for sure." He squinted at me across the buggy seat. "Why'd you have to lean out like that?"

"*What?*" I didn't know when I'd been so mad. "This is my fault? It's my fault *you* don't know how to drive?"

Eli scratched at the dirt with the toe of a polished boot. "Well, I'll, uh, get your bags."

Maybe this was his way of saying he was sorry, but I wasn't having it. "I'll get them myself!" I spat.

We both made a dive for the handle of Ma's valise. Eli pulled, I pulled . . . and that rickety old valise, like it wanted to torment me, popped open. Out tumbled shifts, stockings, petticoats, and even my bloomers. All my girl things, lying right out in the road.

A strangled noise—something like "Errp"—came out of my mouth. For a second I was frozen with mortification. Then I sprang to life, snatching up my belongings, dirt and all. I caught a petticoat just as the breeze tossed it into the air. I bundled everything together and stuffed the wad into the valise, avoiding even a glance in Eli's direction and wishing with all my might that I could bolt right back to my own sod house. Instead, I put the valise in the buggy, fetched my carpet bag, and climbed back on. What choice did I have?

Eli shook the reins. "Did you get all your . . . things?" I stole a peek at him, pretty sure I saw a wicked gleam under his dark lashes.

"Yes!" I barked, feeling a hot blush crawl up my neck. I tossed my head, folded my hands together, and stared straight ahead. From now on, I would simply ignore Eli Lewis, I resolved. I had more important things to think about than cheeky Kiowa boys.

After what seemed like hours, we rolled through the town of Prince Albert, which turned out to be just a fancy train depot, a cattle yard, and a pretty stone church. Then the buggy turned away from the railroad tracks and climbed a little rise. For Kansas, it was a hill. Fields of yellow-green wheat stretched away on both sides of the road. Farther off I saw some black dots that were probably cattle, some white dots that were probably sheep, and some buildings that were probably barns.

"This is a really big claim," I said, forgetting my resolve. "Whose is it?"

"It's Mr. Ashford's, and it's not a *claim*," Eli said. "Mr. Ashford's not a *homesteader*. I heard he bought this land from the railroad. Rich people don't have to homestead, you know."

"Well, obviously," I said with a toss of my head. Then I realized how foolish that sounded. What was *obvious* was that I didn't know what I was talking about. Why did this obnoxious boy get me confused? Why couldn't I talk to him without getting mad, or making him mad, or sounding like an idiot?

Hopefully, at Ashford Manor a *groom* and a *housemaid* wouldn't run into each other.

Chapter 7

Eli stopped the buggy in front of a grand house built of limestone as yellow as bricks of butter. Gracious, Ashford Manor was big. But wait, the "house" had barn doors, and horses stood in the yard—it was a *stable.* Just beyond it was an even grander building made of the same yellow limestone. I stared, bug-eyed. I had never seen a manor before, but this was the most manor-ish building I could imagine. It was three stories tall, with rows of real glass windows that caught the sun like diamonds. It made the Grand Paris Hotel look like a shack.

"You, uh, going to get out?" Eli said.

"Of course!" Before I completely lost my nerve, I grabbed my bags and jumped out of the buggy. I guessed we were at the back of the manor, so I marched along a gravel path to the front, my knees shaking and my heart hammering like a woodpecker.

I climbed onto the front porch and stood at the door, which seemed to be ten feet tall. *Do it, Cabby,* I ordered myself, lifting a shaking hand toward the polished brass doorknocker.

"No, no!" called a voice. My hand froze. A man stood behind a low stone wall off to the side of the house, waving a hoe. "Not that way!" he yelled. "Go in the back door!"

What, I wasn't good enough for the front door? My face burning, I hightailed it back where I had come from. Eli was still there, unbuckling Georgiana's harness. "Back door!" he called.

"Well, thank you very much!" I tried to sound sarcastic, but my voice came out in a squeak.

The back door flew open and Mrs. Shaw bustled out, wearing a white apron over a drab brown dress, her arms dusted to the elbows with flour. I hadn't noticed before how short and stout she was, like a barrel with a round ball for a head. She moved pretty fast for a barrel, though. "Merciful 'eavens!" she exclaimed, throwing up her hands. "Didn't I say I wanted a *clean* girl? Wot a fright you look—'ave you been rolling in the dirt?"

It wasn't too far from the truth. I put a hand to my head. One braid had come unpinned and hung down my back. My dress was gritty with dirt from the road, all thanks to Eli Lewis. "No, I . . ."

"Come along then," Mrs. Shaw ordered, not letting me finish. I followed her into a kitchen almost as big as my house, with a huge stove, shiny pots hanging from hooks, and loads of cupboards and cabinets. And so clean. I would be afraid to touch anything.

"All washing up's to be done in the scullery," Mrs. Shaw said. "You'll find your soft soap in that tin and your blacking polish in that one. You must black the stove every morning and scour the copper pans every week—do you 'ear me, girl?"

"Yes, Ma'am." Actually, her words pinged off my mind

like hailstones. She was talking way too fast.

Just then a man came in, the one who had waved his hoe at me. He had a long face, turned-down eyes, and deep creases around his mouth, giving him a mournful look. He inspected me up and down, set a basket of beans on the table, and sighed. "She tried to go in the front door. Chances are, she'll steal the silver."

"What?" I said, "I would n—"

"We'll keep an eye on 'er, won't we, Mr. Shaw," Mrs. Shaw said, nodding as if the man—her husband, apparently—had said something very wise. I felt guilty, even though I hadn't done anything wrong.

"Now, girl, 'ere's the bucket for well water, and that one's for dirty water," Mrs. Shaw went on. She talked so fast that before I could take in one thing, she had said three things more. "You'll find all your brushes in this closet and rags in that box. On no account are you to sing or whistle in the 'ouse, and if you meet Lady Ashford, don't forget to curtsey. You're to wear your black dress and cap at all times, mind you. Lunch is at one o'clock, tea at four, and dinner at seven . . ."

She hustled out of the kitchen, and I followed her down a hallway sprinkled with delicate little tables, past a room with leather chairs and a huge, glass-eyed buffalo head on the wall, and past another room with potted plants and a piano. She didn't slow down until she had trotted up a wide, polished staircase to a second-floor hallway, where she stopped, panting. "Lord Ashford, Lady Ashford," she announced breathlessly. "And Edgar, Arthur, Ambrose, George, and Nigel. Nigel's the youngest."

"What? Where?" I had been looking out the window

---

at the top of the stairs, wishing myself outside, anyplace but here. I felt like that poor buffalo—dirty and shaggy, an outdoor beast captured and forced indoors. My knees shook, my arms ached from carrying my bags, and my brain buzzed, overstuffed with information.

"'Ere," Mrs. Shaw said, pointing at a photo on the wall. In it, a tall, proud-looking man and a lady all in lace sat in fancy chairs. Four boys stood around them, and a fifth boy in a sailor suit—Nigel, I supposed—leaned on his mother's knee.

"That's a lot of boys," I said, since Mrs. Shaw seemed to want me to say something. I wished she would get to the here's-where-you-can-take-a-little-rest part.

Mrs. Shaw smiled proudly. I think it was the first time I had seen her smile. "And there's meself and Mr. Shaw." She pointed to two tiny figures in another framed photograph. They were dressed in black, standing in line with other black-dressed folks in front of a stone castle with plenty of towers and things.

"What's that place?" I asked.

"Oh, that's Stonehill, Lord Ashford's estate in England."

"That's Nigel's—I mean Mr. Ashford's—*house*?"

"Not *'is,* exactly. Primogeniture, you know."

"Primo . . . what?"

Mrs. Shaw stopped smiling. "Are you going to stand 'ere asking questions all day, missy?" Which was unfair, because she was the one who had shown me the picture. She trotted off again. "'Ere is Milady's room, and Mr. Ashford's room, and the guest rooms and the bathroom . . ."

I stopped trying to take it all in, although I did check

the bathroom for a gold-plated tub. Nope, just a big, white porcelain one. It would take buckets and buckets of water for someone to fill it—for *me* to fill it, I reckoned.

Mrs. Shaw turned a corner and hustled up a narrow staircase to the third floor. Finally, she stopped walking. "This one's *your* room."

I stepped into the small room. It had a washstand, a small dresser, and a bed with a clean white bedspread. Was it all for me? An entire bed? An entire *room?*

"There's a dress and apron and cap for you on the 'ook," Mrs. Shaw said. 'Urry up and change now, there's work to be done." She bustled back down the hall.

Slowly, like in a dream, I dropped my bags on the floor, pulled off my shoes and dress, and lifted the too-wide black dress off its hook. It was made of heavy cotton, thick as canvas. Someone bigger had worn it before me, and there were white stains under the arms from her sweat. Yuck.

Holding my breath, I slid into the hideous dress and buttoned it up. I tied on the bibbed apron, put on the frilled cap with two streamers down the back, and stepped to the mirror over the washstand. A stranger dressed in black stared back at me. She looked pale and scared, wild hair escaping from her cap, and one cheek smudged with dirt. Could that stranger be *me?*

I swiped at my face, tucked in my hair. Then I fished in my carpetbag for the one piece of jewelry I owned, a brooch with a blue stone. The metal was only pewter, and the stone probably glass, but I loved the brooch because Pa had given it to me. He said it made me look like a duchess.

I pinned the brooch on the ugly black dress, lifted my chin, and marched down the stairs.

Chapter 8

O
h great, I was lost. Which way was the kitchen? I picked one direction and wandered into a room so refined Emmeline would have fainted. There were fringed rugs, paintings in gold frames, sparkling glass lamps, velvet-covered sofas, and fancy needlepoint chairs with spindly legs. All that stuff would have filled our house to the brim, but this room was huge, like a lake with islands of furniture.

I remembered the boarding house in Cleveland. Mostly, I hated that place, how we had to share one room and ate boiled mutton at a table crowded with men. But sometimes Emmeline and I would sneak down to the parlor early in the morning, before anyone else was up. It was naughty, but we would jump from chair to sofa to chair, pretending they were islands in the ocean. "Don't touch the floor, or the sharks will get you!" I'd shout.

A little jumping wouldn't hurt *this* stuffy room. I hiked up the hem of the black dress, planning my first leap.

"Where are your *shoes*?" said a stern voice.

I spun around, somehow managing not to squeal in shock. In a deep velvet chair sat the most majestic person I had ever seen. She wore a midnight-blue silk dress festooned with jet beads. She had a thin, pale face, very haughty-looking, and blue-gray eyes. Her white hair was piled on top of her head, held by silver combs.

I let the skirt of the dress fall. "M-my shoes?"

The lady drummed her jeweled fingers on the arm rests.

"They're upstairs, in . . . in the room." I couldn't bring myself to say "my room."

"Well, put them on."

I had never heard of wearing shoes inside. I didn't even wear them outside, except in town. But things were different at manors, apparently. "Okay," I said with a shrug.

The old lady shuddered. "You are to say, 'Yes, Milady.' 'Okay' is vulgar."

Milady . . . My Lady? This was the Ladyship!

"Okay—I mean, yes, Milady." So this was Lady Ashford—too ancient to be Nigel's wife, so she must be his ma. Wouldn't Emmeline love to know that!

Just then I remembered I was supposed to curtsey. Sweeping one bare foot behind the other and pulling the black dress out on both sides, I bent down so deep I almost kissed the floor. A top-notch curtsey, in my opinion, even if I was inexperienced in the art.

But Lady Ashford was not impressed. "Stop that preposterous display. Hasn't Mrs. Shaw explained decorum to you? You *are* the new servant, I take it?"

Servant? I straightened up, touching the brooch at my collar. "No, Milady. I'm not a servant." I met her steely eyes for just a second. "I'm a housemaid," I said, feeling my face burn with pride. *Actually, I'm a homesteader,* I added silently, not daring to say the words aloud. *I'm only here because of the grasshoppers. Because my family needs the money.*

"I trust you'll remember a *housemaid's* place," Lady Ashford snapped. She picked up the book on her lap. "You are dismissed."

Maybe I was supposed to curtsey again, but I almost didn't care. This old lady was not the Queen of America, after all. I turned to leave the room, but just then a plump woman with very pink cheeks waddled in, hiding a yawn behind her hand.

"There you are, Sophie," Lady Ashford said. Mrs. Shaw had mentioned something about a Sophie. Milady's maid, she called her. I couldn't imagine why Lady Ashford needed a whole maid to herself.

"*Va chercher mes lunettes,*" Lady Ashford said to Sophie. "*Et mon chale.*"

"*Oui, Madame,*" Sophie said. They were speaking French, for some reason. Ma had taught us that "*oui*" mean "yes." It would probably surprise the Ladyship that Ma used to be a schoolteacher, and I actually knew a thing or two.

Sophie bobbed a tiny curtsey—so that's how it was done—and left the room without even looking at me. Lady Ashford gave me an impatient glare. "I *said* you are dismissed, Polly."

"Oh, my name isn't Polly," I said politely, figuring that old Ladyships got confused about names. "It's Catherine, but you can call me . . ."

Lady Ashford's eyes narrowed. Her look was as cold as ice. "I shall *call you* whatever I please. And I won't have insolence."

My face flamed, and angry words bubbled in my mind. "But I was just . . ."

"Go!"

The word was like a slap. I stumbled out of the room, blinded by tears, and almost crashed into someone in the hall. I hopped out of the way just in time. I was better at hopping than curtseying, fortunately.

"You are?" the person demanded. It was Nigel.

"The new housemaid," I answered dully, sniffing the tears away. He didn't remember me. To an Ashford, apparently, all *servants* looked alike. And maybe all housemaids were "Polly."

Nigel chuckled. "I remember you now . . . You threw something at me, didn't you?"

I lifted my head. It wasn't the friendliest remark, but after Lady Ashford, any crumb of recognition seemed like a feast. Maybe Nigel Ashford wasn't such a bad person after all. And he certainly was handsome. Leaning against the wall, tall and graceful in his linen jacket and perfectly groomed moustache, he looked like an illustration from one of Emmeline's romantic stories.

"I'm Cabby," I said. "Cabby Potts." I wouldn't let *him* call me Polly. Not if I could help it.

"Ah, yes. How is your fair sister?"

I sighed. "Emmeline? She's fine, I guess."

Figured. It wasn't me he was interested in. Only my fair sister.

—Part 2—

A Brilliant Inspiration

Chapter 9

"Took your time, didn't you?" Mrs. Shaw fussed when I found my way to the kitchen. "Almost lunch time, and will you look at this platter!"

She pushed a silver platter into my hands. It looked perfectly fine to me. "Tarnished!" Mrs. Shaw pronounced, plopping a tin of Globe Silver Polish and a rag onto the table. "'Urry up and polish it. No more dawdling."

I sank into the chair and opened the tin of paste without a word. It wasn't even noon, but I'd been scolded a thousand times, or thereabouts. My pride felt stung by a whole army of wasps—Eli Lewis, Mrs. Shaw, Mr. Shaw, that awful Ladyship, and even Nigel, who pretended to be friendly to me but was only interested in Emmeline.

Wait a minute . . . could it be? Was Nigel *interested* in Emmeline? I stared at the platter, tracing the etched lines with my finger, my thoughts swirling. Nigel had kissed her hand and called her "fair." That had to *mean* something. What if . . .?

"Daydreaming, are you?" said Mrs. Shaw, appearing out of nowhere. She thumped a bowl of potatoes on the table. "Get going, girl. I need you to peel these when you're finished."

I dabbed some paste onto the platter and rubbed it

in as energetically as I could. An idea was forming in my mind. A brilliant inspiration, in fact, based on three solid facts. *One,* Emmeline was crazy about Nigel Ashford. *Two,* my sister was the prettiest and nicest girl in Kansas. And *three,* Nigel Ashford was *interested* in her. He had to be—there was no other explanation.

What if Nigel fell in love with Emmeline? That wasn't so ridiculous. I mean, after interest came love, right?

And after love came marriage.

After *that,* we would all be family. Surely Nigel would want to help us out. That was what family was for. You took care of your mother-in-law and father-in-law and sisters-and-brothers-in-law. Nigel had so many cows, he could spare us one or two. He had so many pots and pans, he could give Ma a few—only not those copper-bottom ones that needed scouring all the time. He had so much money, I bet he could buy the stuff we needed with pocket change.

"Careful with that paste!" cried Mrs. Shaw. "Don't you know it comes all the way from London?"

Mr. Shaw came in behind her with an armful of cut flowers. "Likely she doesn't," he said gloomily. "Doesn't know much, I expect."

I didn't argue. I wasn't going to be here long anyway. I just had to push things along between Nigel and my sister, find a way to bring them together, and let true love take its course. *Poof,* all our problems solved. I'd be home well before Christmas.

In the meantime, best not to get myself fired. I polished the platter carefully and peeled all the potatoes lightning fast. Then I scurried back and forth between the kitchen and the dining room, carrying china plates, crystal goblets, linen napkins, and silver forks, spoons, and knives. So much finery in one place, and it was just lunch. At home, lunch was beans and cornbread on tin plates, every single day.

I set the table like Mrs. Shaw told me: five delicate pink-and-white plates placed with the *A* pointing up, five sets of silverware lined up perfectly, five napkins folded into fan shapes and tucked inside the goblets, one huge vase of flowers set exactly in the center of the table. Too fancy for my taste, but Emmeline would have loved it all.

I passed the Ladyship as I carried the last tray of goblets. I froze, praying my skirt covered my bare feet. Somehow I had forgotten to get my shoes. Fortunately, Lady Ashford didn't seem to notice. She walked slowly, leaning on Sophie's shoulder and coughing a little. Since I was in a forgiving mood, I vowed to have kinder thoughts about my sister's future mother-in-law. Maybe she had a cold. Lots of people were grumpy when they had a cold.

Mr. Shaw set a steaming bowl on the dining table, and everything was ready. I stood nervously behind one of the carved wooden chairs, determined to make a good impression on Lady Ashford during lunch. I would mind my table manners and mention Emmeline only if the conversation drifted in that direction. I wouldn't gobble, even though I was starving, and Mrs. Shaw had made ham salad and pickles and sliced peaches and potatoes dripping with butter, and a fluffy, white-flour angel-food cake. There was also sliced beef tongue, which I would definitely skip.

As Sophie and Lady Ashford entered the dining room,

I slipped into my seat. "Milady," I said oh-so-politely, "I *do* hope you're feeling well this afternoon."

Sophie stopped dead. Her eyes widened in horror. "*Ooh-la-la!*"

Lady Ashford clutched at her throat like someone was choking her. "Out!" she gasped. "Get out!"

I jumped from the chair as if something bit me. Just then, I heard voices in the hall, and Nigel strolled into the dining room, followed by a gentleman and two ladies. In a flash I realized my mistake. The extra places at the table were not for Mrs. Shaw, Mr. Shaw, and me. They were for Mr. Ashford's guests.

Servants did not eat in the dining room.

I bolted from the room, found a side door, and blundered outside, mindlessly following the gravel path toward the back of the house.

How was I supposed to know I couldn't eat in the dining room? In my part of Kansas, hired help ate meals with the family. When Pa hired Bub Skyler to help dig our well, and when our neighbors, the Nybergs, hired Emmeline to help with the new baby, everybody ate together. Folks were just folks. But things were different at Ashford Manor. *People* were different. "Just folks" didn't seem to apply, especially with the Ladyship.

I moped over to a wooden tower with a windmill on top. A distant part of my brain noticed the whoosh of the spinning blades, the up-and-down motion of a rod, the water trickling into a cistern. I'd heard about this new-fangled way to bring water from the ground, but at the moment I wasn't interested.

I leaned against the windmill tower, letting the

June breeze catch the ribbons on my cap. I felt like the dumbest girl in Kansas, and no breeze could blow my humiliation away. So much for my brilliant inspiration. Nigel Ashford wouldn't even eat in the same room as a housemaid. Was he going to marry a housemaid's sister? I kicked at a leg of the tower.

Just then Eli Lewis strolled up. Great, the last person I wanted to see. Or one of the last. "Hey, Cabby, you look different," he said.

"You don't say," I muttered. I was in no mood for comments on my housemaiding attire.

Eli shook his head and splashed water from the cistern onto his face. "I didn't mean anything . . . Is it time for lunch?"

Hot suspicion shot through my veins. Maybe he'd spied on me while I made a fool of myself, trying to eat with the Ashfords. "How should I know?" I snapped.

Eli stared at me like I'd gone insane. Then he shrugged, shook the water from his face, and walked to the back door. A skinny bald man and two dusty-look-ing boys in overalls strolled over from the stable and followed him inside.

Another stupid mistake. The "servants," I understood now, were supposed to eat together in the kitchen. And if I didn't get back inside to help, Mrs. Shaw would bite my head off.

Somehow, I endured my first lunch at Ashford Manor, served on ordinary earthenware plates. The boys, I found out, were field hands, and the skinny bald man was Mr. Hiram Rouse, the farm manager. During lunch,

Mr. Rouse had a lot to say: how wheat was better suited to the Kansas climate than corn, how Mr. Ashford's Angus cattle would fetch a good price, that sort of thing. It was interesting, actually, but I was too rattled to pay proper attention. *Don't make a mistake, Cabby. Don't even look at that aggravating boy.*

But lecturing myself didn't work. When Mrs. Shaw asked me to slice the bread, for some reason I picked up her sharp knife and sliced right into a rolled-up towel. "Are you daft, girl?" Mrs. Shaw shouted, grabbing the knife from my hand.

"I expect she is," said Mr. Shaw sadly. Out of the corner of my eye, I saw Eli shaking with laughter.

That was it: Eli Lewis was my sworn enemy number one. Well, maybe number two. Number one was definitely the Ladyship.

Chapter 10

Things did not improve next morning. "That's a floor broom, not a carpet broom!" scolded Mrs. Shaw. And, "Clean the smudge off your apron!" And, "Don't you know a spoon from a fork?"

I said "Yes, Ma'am" and "Sorry, Ma'am" so many times I felt like a parrot. Maybe Polly *was* a good name for me.

It was almost a relief when Mrs. Shaw sent me upstairs. Sophie took care of Lady Ashford's bedroom, but I had to make Nigel's bed, pick up his dirty clothes, *and* empty his chamber pot, which I considered most unfair. I mean, I used a chamber pot if I had to relieve myself in the night, but I wouldn't expect someone else to empty it.

I tackled the bed and dirty clothes first. It was amazing how many shirts, trousers, and stockings Nigel Ashford had strewn around his room. When I couldn't put off the chamber pot any longer, I held my nose and slid the china bowl from under the bed. No *unmentionables* inside, at least.

Then I had an idea. Why carry the stinky pot all the way downstairs? What a waste of time. And the window was right here.

I opened the window, thrust out the pot, tipped it

over, and . . .

"*Pollee! Quelle horreur!*" a voice shrieked. Oh, no! Sophie—and Lady Ashford—stood right below me. Lady Ashford stared wordlessly as the contents of the pot splashed inches from the hem of her dress. Sophie screeched as if someone was trying to kill her.

I pulled the pot back in and slammed the window shut. "Dang it all!" This was the worst curse I had ever uttered, but it was the right time for it.

I would hear about this escapade from Mrs. Shaw, I was sure.

And I did. No point repeating what she said, except that "Don't go dumping chamber pots out of windows" was added to the daily scolding. "Or you'll get thrown out too," Mrs. Shaw added grimly.

The only thing that got me through the next week was the thought of Sunday, my first half-day off. But when the day finally arrived, I woke up feeling as glum as an owl in the rain. Unless I grew a pair of wings, I couldn't get home and back before two o'clock, when I had to resume my duties. What good was time off if I couldn't go home?

I watched through my bedroom window as a polished black carriage, like a giant apple on wheels, rolled away from the stable. Nigel and the Ladyship were inside, I assumed, along with Mr. and Mrs. Shaw, on their way to church in Prince Albert. I couldn't see who was driving the pair of horses, but I assumed it was Eli. Good, enemy number one and number two were out of the way. Maybe I'd visit the stable, see if that would cheer me up.

Wearing one of my own dresses and no shoes, I

strolled to the stable and leaned on the fence enclos-
ing the corral. Three sleek, well-fed horses stood in the
enclosure. If I was home, our horses Lightning and Bolt—
who were slow as snails, despite their names—might be
hauling us to church to hear a traveling preacher. I'd be
giggling with Emmeline, reminding Jesse not to muss his
Sunday clothes, and arguing with Orin about something
or other. The Nybergs' wagon might catch up with us,
all their yellow-haired kids crammed in the wagon bed.
"Good morgoon!" Pa would call, butchering the Swedish
words on purpose, and the Nyberg kids would laugh.

I missed being on the prairie. I missed Pa. I missed
my sister and brothers so much it was like an actual pain.
I even missed Ma, or Ma before she turned mean and
decided to send me away. Ma had always been as brisk
and practical as a new straw broom—as prickly too. But
she used to smile occasionally, before . . .

"Stop that, you demon!" said a voice. It was the farm
manager, Mr. Rouse, who lived with Eli above the stable.
He ducked away from the bared teeth of the enormous
black stallion in the corral. "You nip me, you'll be sorry!"
He saw me staring and laughed. "Cabby, meet Admiral.
Very important bloodlines, you know," he said, pinching
his nose and sounding just like Nigel.

I laughed too. "He *is* a beauty."

Mr. Rouse shook his head. "An English thoroughbred is good for nothing out here, except racing, maybe.
Admiral spooks at his own shadow, and he's mean as
heck. Give me one of these cow ponies any day." He
pointed at a small white horse with one black leg; it
reminded me of the spotted pony at Mrs. Lewis's livery

stable. "This one's nimble and smart, practically reads your mind."

The pony trotted over to me, and I stroked his soft muzzle through the fence. He was cute, for sure. I liked the way his ears flicked back and forth.

Mr. Rouse saddled his own brown horse and rode off. Once he was out of sight, I slipped through the gate and into the corral. Admiral was safely on the other side, biting at the top rail of the fence. I patted the white-and-black pony's neck and let him rub his head against my shoulder. Then I hoisted my skirt and petticoat, stepped on the bottom rail of the fence, and straddled the pony's back. Nothing to it.

What harm would it do to walk the little horse around the corral? Nudging his sides with my bare heels, I coaxed him into a walk and practiced turning him with my knees. I'd ridden Lightning and Bolt that way, only they were as wide as barrels compared to this fellow. Round and round the corral we went.

Actually . . . what harm would it do to take the tiniest walk on the prairie? The pony needed exercise, no doubt. And I . . . I needed some *freedom* after the week I'd had.

I glanced around. No one in sight. I steered the pony out of the corral, closed the gate carefully behind me, and looked around again. All clear. I was *borrowing*, not stealing . . . but I felt a mite anxious until we were out in the open grassland, the little horse prancing along like today was his birthday. The wind blew hard, tossing the grasses, making ripples and currents in a bright green ocean. Jackrabbits sat up to watch us, black-tipped ears poking above the stems. For the first time in what seemed like forever, I could really breathe.

I could tell the little fellow wanted to run. "Go on, boy!" I bellowed, grabbing a handful of mane. He broke into a gallop, and I clamped my knees against his sides. "Whoo-ee!" We pounded over the prairie. Finally he pulled up at the edge of a shallow gully, and I slid off, the breath sucked right out of my lungs.

A creek ran through the bottom of the gully, and I let the pony go down. He huffed at the water, took a long drink, then lay right down and rolled, three white legs and one black kicking into the air. I laughed out loud.

Here by the sparkling water, with birds flitting every-where, inspirations of all sort seemed more likely to work out. Maybe my matchmaking plan wasn't so crazy. Stranger things had happened. In fact, in the stories Emmeline liked to read, unlikely romances happened all the time. Hadn't Count Roderigo fallen in love with penniless Cecilia in "The Bride of Madrid"? Of course Cecilia turned out to be a Spanish princess in disguise, with jewels sewn into the hem of her dress. But never mind that. Once he got to know my sister, Nigel would be smitten with her, jewels or no jewels. The snooty old Ladyship might oppose the match, but true love would overcome all obstacles. Hopefully.

I hiked up my skirt and waded in the creek, holding the pony by the halter. "That Lady Ashford. She's as sour as a pickled lemon!" I told him, and he snorted sympa-thetically. Just then, an answering snort made me jump. A wide black head stared down at us from the lip of the gully. Good gracious, a buffalo! I scrambled up the other bank, pulling the pony with me, my heart pounding.

Wait, it wasn't a buffalo. The buffalo were gone from the prairie. The black head on the other side of the creek belonged to a *cow*. But this big, muscular animal was nothing like the scrawny Texas longhorns I was used to.

More black cattle—Angus, I think Mr. Rouse called them—milled around, cropping the green grass contentedly. They didn't look dangerous. Still, I felt shaky. Time to go.

I scrambled onto the pony and turned around and around. That's when it hit me: I had no idea where I was. The prairie stretched away in all directions, rolling over little dips and swells. No houses, no trees, no landmarks. Just me on my little pony, a herd of big black animals, and the wide open plain.

I swallowed hard, fighting off the panic that rose in my throat. I'd heard countless stories: people eaten by wolves, swallowed by snowstorms. Children wandering for days, falling into wells . . . The prairie was deceptive, the way it looked flat but was actually creased by gullies and dips that could lead you astray.

Foolish, foolish, Cabby. The first rule every Kansas kid learned was: don't get lost.

Chapter 11

I tried to steady my nerves. Snow wasn't likely, and I couldn't be too far from the manor. "Right, boy?" I asked the pony, my voice tight and squeaky. He pawed at the grass, and I remembered what Mr. Rouse had said about my little friend: "he practically reads your mind."

"Go home?" I said. The pony dropped his head and took a mouthful of grass. I smacked my heels into his sides. "Go home!" He started to walk. "Please, please, go the right way." The pony nodded his head—or possibly I just imagined it.

On we plodded, step, step, step through the swishing grasses. I didn't dare hurry him. If I returned Mr. Ashford's horse covered in sweat, it would be obvious someone had ridden him. It was agony.

Hours later, or so it seemed, I saw Ashford Manor on its little rise. Whew! I clapped the pony with my heels, and he trotted the rest of the way to the stable . . . arriving at the very moment the Ashfords' carriage pulled up from the opposite direction.

Oh, no.

I was caught.

Eli ran out of the stable. So he hadn't been the one

driving the carriage. He'd been in the stable all along; maybe he'd seen me ride off on Nigel's horse.

Nigel—he was the one driving—hopped down from the seat at the front of the carriage, his face tight with fury.

In horrible slow motion, I slid off the pony's back, wishing the ground would swallow me up. "I-I'm sorry," I stuttered.

But Nigel turned on Eli. "What kind of groom are you?"

Eli said nothing.

"You let housemaids take pleasure rides on my Indian pony?"

I couldn't believe it. Eli Lewis was getting blamed for what I did.

"Well, boy?"

In the long silence that followed, I realized what I *should* do. I *should* speak up, tell the truth, admit that Eli didn't *let* me do anything. I had taken Nigel's horse without permission. I had known all along it was wrong.

But if I confessed, I might get fired. Nigel would certainly be soured on me, and he might never fall in love with Emmeline . . . I held on tight to the pony's halter, my brain swirling with conflicting thoughts.

Finally, "I'm sorry, sir," Eli muttered, staring at the ground.

I let out the breath I'd been holding with a *whoosh.* Eli hadn't told on me. Somehow the storm had passed—over me, anyway.

Just then the carriage door opened, and my heart stopped. I had forgotten about the Ladyship. But it was

Mrs. Shaw, not Lady Ashford, who climbed down from the carriage. She barged over, grabbed me by the wrist, and half-dragged me toward the house, fussing the whole way. "I don't care if that boy let you do it, you should 'ave known better. Riding the Master's 'orse, indeed! Who do you think you are, missy?"

Pa calls me a duchess, I wanted to say—but didn't, of course.

Mrs. Shaw pulled me into the kitchen and let the door bang behind us. "It's lucky for you Milady went to the Banisters' after church, or you would catch it!"

"Are . . . are you going to tell her?" A lecture from Mrs. Shaw was bad enough; Lady Ashford's icy wrath would be worse.

"Certainly not," Mrs. Shaw said. "Who do you think gets blamed if a 'ousemaid misbehaves?" She picked up a spoon and wagged it in my face. "You're to stay away from that stable, you understand?"

I gulped and nodded; I had no choice. But it stung. The little white-and-black horse was my best friend at Ashford Manor. My only friend.

I hurried up the stairs. All things considered, I had gotten off pretty lightly. But I felt heavy, like a weight was pressing on me. I pulled off my dress and looked out the window in my shift; I could see Eli in the corral, sponging off one of the carriage horses. Even from here I could make out the tense lines in his back. *You're a coward,* said a voice in my head. *What if he gets in real trouble because of you?*

So what? said another voice. *He got you in trouble too, letting you show up at Ashford Manor covered in dirt. It's arithmetic; you're equal now.*

I turned away from the window, a bitter taste in my mouth, and spent the rest of my time off in my room.

Helpful, not troublesome. A model housemaid. By tea time, that's what I'd decided to be. I had escaped the fire that morning, but I couldn't break any more rules. Not if I wanted to push my matchmaking scheme along.

"We've got company for tea," Mrs. Shaw said when I slipped into the kitchen, my hair combed, my cap on straight, my shoes laced all the way up. She pulled a tray of triangle-shaped cakes from the oven, her face shiny with sweat. "Sir Roger and Lady Margaret Banister, and the young lady, Miss . . . Miss . . ."

"Lavinia Peacock, niece of Lady Banister," said Mr. Shaw. "She's visiting the Banisters from England."

"Ah, yes," said Mrs. Shaw. She shoveled the hot scones onto a tea tray. "Let's see, the Master, Milady, the Banisters, Miss Peacock, that makes . . ."

"It makes five," I said. I knew not to count housemaids now.

"Hmmp," said Mrs. Shaw, counting on her fingers to check my math. "Take this to the front porch, and *don't spill.*"

"Yes, Ma'am," I said, meek as a lamb. I took the loaded tea tray and hurried around the side of the house. Out front, Nigel and his guests—I recognized them from my horrible first lunch at Ashford Manor—strolled around the perfectly mowed lawn with long mallets in their hands. They took turns whacking wooden balls, rolling them through wire hoops. It was a game I had seen in a magazine: parquet, croquet, something like that.

I stood with the tray in my hands, trying to imagine Emmeline out there, laughing with those people. It was a stretch for the imagination, let me tell you. In the Potts household, we didn't play lawn games while other people served us tea. We didn't even have a lawn.

There was a shriek of laughter. A skinny gray dog had just picked up Nigel's ball and galloped off with it. The young lady seemed to find this hilarious. She was a yellow-haired, frothy kind of person, wearing a white dress with a blue sash and layers and layers of ruffles. She wore tiny white gloves and tiny kid-leather boots. "Isn't that just *too* funny!" she squealed.

The older gentleman—Sir Roger Banister, I guessed—laughed too. "That will teach you to bet money on croquet, Nigel, my boy." He had a lazy, sarcastic way of talking, like everything bored him.

Nigel smacked his mallet into the ground, muttering something under his breath. But he perked up when the girl handed him her parasol, which was ruffled and lined with blue silk to match her sash. Nigel had to lean in close to keep her in the shade, much too close for my liking. Who was this girl?

"Polly, bring the tea tray at once!" called Lady Ashford from the porch.

I hustled to the porch and managed to deliver the tray without spilling anything. The croquet players dropped their mallets and gathered on porch chairs, ignoring me completely. I stood still as a post while the Ashfords sipped their tea and munched their scones, my feet slowly going numb in the too-tight shoes—a problem

I could have avoided by going barefoot, but I was being a model housemaid.

The yellow-haired girl, it turned out, had a lot to say. "Ah, what a view you have here, Nigel!" She waved her arm toward the horizon, almost knocking into Lady Ashford's teacup. "Look at all that . . . space! The American prairie is magnificent!"

"Magnificent if you like looking at nothing but grass all day," said Sir Roger with a yawn. "In the summer it's hot as blazes and in the winter it's bloody cold."

"Roger!" said the woman sitting next to him. Lady Banister, I figured. She sat so erect and proper I figured her corset was too tight; her big nose and severe, squinty eyes reminded me of a snapping turtle.

"Pardon my language," Sir Roger said, nodding at Lavinia. "But it's true. Imagine all this covered with snow, with the wind whipping across it. There's nothing to stop the wind before the Rocky Mountains."

The girl shivered and leaned close to Nigel, batting her eyelashes. "Well, at least you have a snug house to keep you warm." She bit into another scone. "I do *adore* your house, Nigel," she mumbled with her mouth full.

What a flirt she was. And in spite of her fancy clothes and refined way of talking, she had bad manners.

Lady Banister gave Nigel a meaningful look and patted her niece's hand. "You could get accustomed to America, couldn't you, my dear?"

Lavinia giggled. "Everything depends on the company you're with." She peeked at Nigel, and he actually blushed.

Oh, no.

This girl *wanted to marry Nigel Ashford.* It was so

obvious even I could see it. I rocked back on my heels like someone had run into me.

What chance did my sister have against the little Peacock? Emmeline didn't have a silk-lined parasol or a big house in England. She didn't own little white gloves. She would never be invited to Ashford Manor for tea and croquet.

"Pay attention, Polly!" Lady Ashford said sharply. "Take the tea tray."

I lurched forward on my frozen feet, grabbed the tray, and staggered backwards.

Crash!

Chapter 12

"Help!" shrieked Lavinia, like I had shot her.

"Oh, for pity's sake," muttered Nigel, picking a shard of china out of his trouser cuff.

Sir Roger laughed. "I told you American girls were clumsy, Nigel."

Lady Ashford's voice was quiet but terrible. "Pick up that mess, and be quick about it." I knelt down and piled the china fragments onto the tray, my hands shaking. I could only imagine what Mrs. Shaw would say.

"Six dollars and thirty cents," is what she said. That's how much one china teapot and two china cups cost. That's how much money would be *subtracted from my pay.*

Three weeks and one day. That's how long I had to work before I earned a penny at Ashford Manor.

I couldn't believe it. The Ashfords had plenty of money—what was six dollars and thirty cents to them? "It's not fair!" I cried. "It was an accident."

Mrs. Shaw took my face between her two rough hands. "Never say it's not fair. Never! It's our lot, and we don't complain about it."

Our lot? The lot of a *servant*?

"It's 'ard, lass," Mrs. Shaw went on, her round face softening. "It does seem unfair, sometimes. One of Milady's dinner dresses costs five times wot I make in a year. But you get used to it."

I turned my face away, everything in me protesting silently. *No, I will never get used to it. I might have to work here a while, but I will never become a servant.*

"You're fortunate, anyway," Mrs. Shaw said. "It was the second-best china, and only two cups broke."

I didn't feel fortunate, let me tell you. Not only did I owe the Ashfords money instead of the other way around, Nigel was going to marry that awful Lavinia Peacock. I just knew it. She visited all the time. Sometimes she and Nigel played the piano, Lavinia banging away like she wanted to break the instrument. Or they played cards with the Banisters, Lady Banister making sly remarks about how pleasant life in America was. Other times Nigel visited her. I heard talk of lawn tennis and picnics and a game called cricket. Nigel didn't act all mushy with Miss Lavinia; he didn't quote poetry or gaze into her eyes, at least that I saw. But who knew what true love, English style, looked like?

"Miss Peacock's got 'er sights on our Master, 'asn't she?" I heard Mr. Shaw ask his wife one day.

"I expect so," Mrs. Shaw said. "From wot I 'eard, the girl's got quite a fortune, but 'er father's only a baronet. She's after Nigel's title, I'll wager."

"We shall have two mistresses at Ashford Manor before long, 'eaven 'elp us," Mr. Shaw sighed. Good thing I wasn't holding a teapot right then, because I might have dropped it on the floor. I hadn't even thought about Lavinia Peacock becoming mistress of Ashford Manor. It was an idea too horrible for words.

I dragged through the days, going through the motions of housemaiding, as miserable as . . . well, as a farm girl stuck inside, just praying she wouldn't break anything else, while the sunshine called through the open windows. I felt like all the color was seeping out of me, that soon I would be as pale and bug-eyed as one of those crayfishes that live under the rocks in the stream.

One broiling late-June afternoon, Mrs. Shaw sat me by the kitchen window with a pile of frayed linen napkins to hem. It should have been an easy job, just a simple whip-stitch, but soon I was so frustrated I wanted to scream. My stitches wouldn't line up in the same direction, and the needle kept slipping in my sweaty fingers. How I wished Emmeline would walk into the room. "What a mess you're making, Cabbage," she would laugh. She'd take over the mending and I'd go out to the garden or the fields. I wasn't afraid of hard work, but this fussy kind of job drove me crazy.

I stared out the window. I wondered if Orin had learned to crack a whip and if Jesse's loose tooth had finally come out. I wondered if Ma's chickens were laying and how much she was getting for the eggs. I wondered if Knee-High's cat was still hissing at Emmeline and if she had managed to read the last installment of "The Bride of Madrid" in Mrs. Buchanan's magazine. I wondered if our corn was still growing strong and if Pa was keeping the weeds down without me to help.

"Cabby!" Mrs. Shaw said. "Can't you keep your mind on your work for five minutes, girl?"

I picked up the next napkin, my vision blurred with tears. I wanted to fling those dratted napkins on the floor, run out the door, and not stop running until I was at my own sod house.

But what good would that do? Ma and Pa would only send me back. I blinked hard and steadied the needle in my fingers. The whipstitch: round and round, round and round.

The next day was laundry day. I set up my tubs in the tiny sliver of shade next to the house. I had to scrub the clothes on the washing board, slosh them in the rinsing basin, squeeze them through the mangle, and hang them on the line, which wasn't so different from laundry at home—except that the Ashfords had enough dirty laundry for an entire city. It was sweaty work, and my fingers quickly turned to wrinkled prunes, but at least I was outside, and I felt my mood lift. "Oh, Susanna, don't you cry for me," I whistled, but stopped when Eli Lewis plodded around the corner of the house, lugging a heavy tub.

"Mrs. Shaw said bring fresh water," he mumbled, looking sort of in my direction but refusing to meet my eyes. We hadn't spoken a word to each other, beyond necessary things like "pass the salt," since the day I "borrowed" the pony.

Eli dumped the old wash water out, making a black beetle scuttle out of the way. Both of us stared at that beetle like it was the most interesting thing in the world, and suddenly it seemed ridiculous, me and Eli Lewis being enemies. Maybe it was time for him to get over his silly grudge. I opened my mouth to say something along those lines, but what came out was, "I'm sorry."

Eli poured fresh water into the wash basin. "Yeah?"

"I'm sorry I didn't tell Mr. Ashford I took his pony," I babbled. "I didn't want to get in trouble and get fired, but I should have told him."

"You're right about that," Eli muttered.

"I can still tell him now, if you want." I couldn't believe I said that. What if he took me up on it?

A hint of a smile appeared on Eli's face. "Nah. I guess you're in enough trouble. I heard about the china."

I fed a sheet into the mangle, cranking the handle to turn the rollers. "I bet you thought that was hilarious."

"No, I . . ."

"You're always laughing at me! Like in the buggy on the way here, and that time at lunch . . ."

Eli grinned. "When you almost cut a towel in half with the bread knife? That was funny!"

I tried to feel indignant, but I smiled instead. It *was* funny, now that I thought about it.

"And you," Eli said. He put his nose in the air and tossed his head, giving a pretty good imitation of me. "You're always acting so high and mighty."

"I am not!" I felt a warmth in my chest that moved up to my face. Was I blushing? I yanked the sheet out of the mangle and stepped to the clothesline, trying hard *not* to toss my head.

Eli took one end of the sheet. I handed him a clothespin, and he pinned the sheet to the line, both of us squinting against the blinding sun. It was the first time anyone had helped me with anything at Ashford Manor.

"His name is Three-Legs, by the way," Eli said. "The pony. Mr. Ashford bought him from my ma."

"Oh?" I said cautiously. I was still worried I would say something stupid, or offend him with my questions.

"My ma, my *kgou-gkoy*, trains her ponies the Kiowa way," Eli said proudly. "Walks them out in the prairie-dog colony so they learn not to step in holes. That's why you didn't get your neck broke on your little gallop."

I gulped. I wanted to ask how he knew the pony had galloped. I also wanted to know more about his Kiowa mother, and about his father. What happened to Mr. Lewis? But now wasn't the time. "Why do you call the pony Three-Legs?" I asked instead.

"Because he's all white with one black leg. When you look at him in the dark, the black leg sort of disappears." Eli sounded cautious too. We weren't used to this talking thing.

"In a snowstorm, the white legs would disappear. You'd have to call him One-Leg," I said, and Eli smiled. It was nice, just making conversation.

"How do you say 'pony' in Kiowa?" I asked, edging closer to the subject of his family.

Eli scowled. "I have no idea."

I expected he did know. It was odd: one minute he seemed proud of being Kiowa, the next minute he pretended not to know the language.

Eli looked at me, his scowl softening. "Would you go around speaking Kiowa, if you were me?" He picked up another damp sheet and pinned one end to the line.

"Actually, it doesn't matter if I speak Kiowa or not. Folks think I'm a 'dirty Indian' no matter what."

"No they don't!" I sputtered, flinching at the awful phrase. I admired the people of Slocum City, with the exception of Mrs. Snopes, and I didn't like to think of them holding mean, ignorant attitudes.

"You sure, Cabby?"

I remembered someone's comment the day Eli picked me up in town: "He cleans up pretty good . . . considering." But that was a joke, wasn't it?

Just then, a voice called from the stable. "James!" It was Nigel.

I stared at Eli. "He calls you *James*?"

"Um . . . got to go." Eli took off running.

I thought about calling after him—*Lady Ashford calls me Polly!*—but I didn't. I'd tell him sometime, maybe, but not yet. "Eli Lewis is my friend" was still a new idea.

Chapter 13

I scrubbed another sheet, the smile fading from my face. James and Polly. The groom and the housemaid. The thing was, I hardly noticed it any more, being called Polly. By Christmas, would I forget my own name? I dunked the sheet into the rinsing basin and poked at it furiously with my stick.

Just then, I heard somebody screaming, *"Sair-pont! Sair-pont!"* It was Sophie, running my direction in a total tizzy. Face pale, mouth open, she sprinted past me, threw open the back door of the house, and barged inside. *Bang* went the door, slamming behind her.

What in the world?

I walked toward the gravel path where Sophie and Lady Ashford took their daily walk, my stirring stick still in my hand. Lady Ashford stood in the path, waving her cane at something. I started running, my heart in my throat. *Sair-pont* must be . . . yipes, serpent! Lying in front of Lady Ashford was a diamond-patterned snake longer and thicker than my arm, stretched across the path in a lazy *S* shape.

I stopped in my tracks. "Back away, Milady!" I ordered. "Just back off!" How many times had Pa told me: when you see a snake, back off, leave it be. But Lady

Ashford didn't listen. She waved her cane at the snake, irritating it. "Shoo! Shoo!" she commanded.

I heard a terrifying noise, like the sound of fat sizzling in a frying pan, and my knees went weak. A rattler! Its bite could kill. Slowly, the snake gathered into a coil and lifted its head and upper body, its tail shaking like mad. I felt paralyzed, like I was stuck in mud. Any instant, the thing would strike Lady Ashford.

Move, Cabby! I forced my frozen legs into a run and darted toward the snake, sliding the stirring stick under its coils. Just as it lunged toward Lady Ashford, I lifted the wriggling creature into the air and flung it as hard and far as I could over the low garden wall. I dropped the stick, hearing a shrill scream. Good gracious, the screamer was me.

Pounding feet hurried toward us. Mr. Shaw, Mrs. Shaw, Nigel, and Eli came running from different directions, all shouting at once. "Milady!" "Mother!" "Are you hurt?" Taking Lady Ashford's arms, Mr. Shaw and Nigel half-carried her toward the kitchen door, Mrs. Shaw bustling behind. They didn't look back.

Wobbly-legged, I picked up the stirring stick.

"You okay?" someone said. Eli.

I nodded, dazed.

"Was it a rattler?"

I nodded again.

"What did you do, *wash* the thing?" He pointed at my stick.

"No, you idiot. I, uh, threw it over the wall."

Eli whistled. "Threw it over the wall? Not bad!"

This time I knew I was blushing. "I didn't even think

about it. I just . . ."

"For a *girl,* I mean," Eli added.

When I finally finished pegging miles of laundry to the clothesline, I headed inside. Sophie sat at the table, a heap of Lady Ashford's silk dresses in front of her. These delicate dresses had to be spot-washed by hand, using a cut potato to lift the stains. Instead of working, though, Sophie sipped a glass of sherry. I glared at her. I wished I knew the French words for "Why did you run away and leave your mistress to the snake?" She looked back at me, all innocent.

Just then Mrs. Shaw popped out of the pantry, face red, arms full of cans and jars. "There you are, lass. I need you to tidy up in the drawing room. Go on, now."

I found a feather duster and headed to the drawing room, feeling a tad sorry for myself. I was soaked with sweat, my hands were raw and wrinkled, and I was still shaky inside. It wasn't every day I threw snakes over walls.

In the drawing room, Lady Ashford was asleep in her velvet chair, a fan folded in her lap. I tiptoed around, dusting, straightening chairs, and gathering dirty plates and glasses. I picked up two books that lay on the floor near the Ladyship's chair. One had a French title, and the other was called *A Treatise on Consumption.* She sure had curious taste in books.

Lady Ashford stirred, and I quickly set the books on the side table. "Help me up," she commanded in a whisper.

I took the Ladyship's arm—it was so skinny, like a bone encased in silk. She got to her feet with a groan.

"I do want to thank you for dealing with that revolting reptile," she said, pulling a coin from an embroidered drawstring purse. "Here you are."

I thrust both hands behind my back. "No! I mean, no thank you, Milady. That's not why I did it."

Lady Ashford weighed the coin in her hand—it was a dollar piece. For a second I considered grabbing it. What an idiot I was, passing up a whole dollar. But I couldn't change my mind now. I swallowed hard, and Lady Ashford put the coin back in her purse. She shook her head. "Are all American girls like you?"

I couldn't help grinning. It was a strange question, but it was the first time she'd asked me something, something about *myself.* "Most of them are better at sewing, Milady."

She almost smiled. "That will be all, P—"

"*Catherine,*" I said. "Cabby" was probably too much to ask.

Silence.

I bit my lip. Held my breath. Looked hard at the design on the rug.

Lady Ashford cleared her throat. "Very well. Catherine."

I let out my breath and made a perfect curtsey as the Ladyship hobbled out the door. A big part of me regretted giving up the dollar. But another part of me thought I had made a good bargain: my own name back in return for an impulsive act of bravery.

Catherine, not Polly. For that, I would throw a *crocodile* over a wall.

I heard Lady Ashford coughing out in the hall, and a

sudden thought made me pick up one of the books on the side table. My heart sinking, I re-read the title: *A Treatise on Consumption.*

I understood now. Maybe I should have understood earlier.

Consumption. It wasn't just a cold.

There was a consumptive lady at the boarding house in Cleveland, and I remembered the sound of her rattling cough. I remembered how they carried her body down the stairs when she died, two men balancing it like it weighed nothing at all. Consumption was a horrible, wasting disease.

Slowly, I opened the book at Lady Ashford's silver bookmark. "A Prairie Cure" was the chapter title.

"There is no climate more sal . . . salub . . . sa*lu*brious than the great American prairie," I read, mouthing the words. "Dr. Abernathy remarks that he has never heard of consumption among the native inhabitants of the New World . . ."

I wondered who this Dr. Abernathy was, and what made him an expert on the great American prairie and its inhabitants.

"Patients taking the Prairie Cure are to follow a strict regimen of outdoor exercise, which will gradually . . ."

So that was why Lady Ashford had come to Kansas, why she walked outside every day.

I hadn't heard of the prairie curing any diseases, but . . .

The Prairie Cure, let it work, Dear Lord, I added to my prayers that night.

— Part 3 —

A Holiday and a Horse Race

Chapter 14

After my prayers, I went to sleep a little more cheerfully than usual. In one day, I had made some progress with sworn enemy number one *and* number two. But the next morning I woke up sweating in my third-floor bedroom, discouraged again. What did it matter if I was making friends with Eli? Who cared what Lady Ashford called me? I was still a housemaid, still stuck here, and Nigel was still going to marry Lavinia Peacock. What I needed was a miracle.

Later that day, I got one. Maybe not a miracle, but a fortuitous opportunity, dropped into my lap by none other than Miss Peacock herself.

It happened just after lunch. Nigel, Lavinia, and the Banisters were playing cards in the drawing room, something they did a lot. They played for money, and the Banisters were winning. I could tell by the pile of dollar bills in front of Sir Roger.

"Really, Nigel, you shouldn't bid so extravagantly," Lady Banister said as I came into the room with a tray of oysters and crackers.

"Whist is a boring game if you don't bid extravagantly," Nigel griped. He handed Sir Roger a dollar.

Sir Roger laughed, adding the bill to his pile. "Well, I

don't mind taking your money, but won't the paterfamilias disapprove?"

"Paterfamilias"? What was that? Curious, I set down the tray and sauntered to the window, pretending to straighten the drapes.

"Oh, he doesn't care," Nigel said. "He sends my remittance steady as clockwork, and more when I need it."

"Paterfamilias" meant father, I guessed. And "remittance" . . . I had heard the word before, something Knee-High Meacham said the morning I left for Ashford Manor: "He's nothing but a re-re-mittance man." What did Knee-High mean by that?

Sir Roger gathered the bills and tucked them carefully into his shirt pocket. "Well, young man, if you feel the necessity of actually making an income, come and talk to me. The real money around here is in . . ."

I would have liked to know where the real money was, but Lavinia butted in before Sir Roger could finish. "Oh, do stop talking about money," she said. "It's so tiresome." She tossed down her cards with a sigh. "And in my last week in America!"

Really? Her last week? I stole a glance at Nigel, who didn't look one bit heartbroken. Maybe there was no engagement after all. I smiled into the folds of the drapes. Let Miss Lavinia Peacock go back to England and find a husband over there.

"And I still haven't seen a buffalo," Lavinia said. "Or an Indian," she added, as if buffalos and Indians were sort of the same.

"The buffalo are gone, more's the pity," said Sir Roger. "They were jolly sport to hunt. In fact, Nigel's father, Lord Ashford, shot that fellow on the study wall. It was on a hunting trip to America. "

"Yes, too bad about the buffalo," said Nigel. "But if you want to see an Indian, take a look at my groom. He's an Indian, I believe. Or half Indian."

Kiowa. Your groom is Kiowa, not "Indian." And he's a person, not a prize pet, I wanted to say—but didn't. Housemaids did not correct their employers.

"So I've seen *one* Indian, I guess," Lavinia said carelessly. She sighed again. "But I've never seen a genuine Kansas sod house."

I couldn't believe it. Sod houses had nothing on grand English manors, but for some reason Lavinia wanted to see one. Here was the very opportunity I needed to bring Nigel and Emmeline together, now that Lavinia was conveniently stepping out of the way. I took a shaky breath. "*I* live in a sod house."

Everybody looked at me in astonishment. It was like the draperies had spoken.

"I can take you to see it," I said. "It's extremely genuine."

"Oh, can we go?" Lavinia cried. "It will be my last American adventure!"

Minutes later, I was headed toward home in Nigel's fancy four-wheeled closed carriage pulled by a pair of matching horses. Strictly speaking, I wasn't *in* the carriage—my spot was an outside seat, more like a shelf, at the back. Sir Roger, Lady Margaret, and Lavinia sat inside, and Nigel drove. I made sure to hang onto the handles as my backside thumped against the hard seat. I wasn't sure anyone would notice if I fell off.

It had been three weeks since Eli drove me to Ashford Manor. Now, I watched that journey unspool in reverse: the manor on its little rise, the town of Prince Albert, then the open prairie with its double-line path through the grasses. I wished I could fly ahead of the carriage to warn Ma, Pa, and Emmeline that we were coming. Instead, I sent a little prayer: *let Nigel and Emmeline hit it off.*

When we arrived in Slocum City, Nigel stopped to water the horses, fortunately for my backside. I hopped off my seat, aware of a lot of curious eyes on the proud horses and gleaming black carriage.

Wouldn't you know it, that busybody Mrs. Snopes scurried up. "Where are you and your fancy gentleman going?" she demanded, the stuffed bird on her hat quivering excitedly.

"Just out to my claim for . . . a visit," I said, trying to sound like this was the most natural thing in the world.

"A visit?" said Mrs. Snopes suspiciously.

"Come up here and give me directions, would you?" Nigel called down to me.

"Got to go," I said, climbing up to the driver's seat at the front of the carriage. Whew. Mrs. Snopes wasn't any taller than I was, but she made me nervous.

As the carriage rolled out of Slocum City, I racked my brain for some way to bring up my sister—to water the seeds of love, so to speak. Maybe there was an interest Nigel and Emmeline had in common. Horses? No. Lawn tennis? No. Cards? No. Piano? Oh dear.

I glanced over at Nigel. If he had love on his mind, he

sure didn't show it. He stretched out his long legs and whistled, occasionally flicking the whip over his horses' backs. "Come on, my beauties!" he shouted. He was driving too fast, in my opinion.

It seemed like only five minutes later when Nigel pulled the horses to a stop in front of my house. I climbed down, nervous as little bird, wishing more than ever that I could have warned my family we were coming.

How tiny my house looked. In spite of Pa's efforts to lay the sod squares straight, one window tilted, and the roof sagged in a couple of spots.

"Oh my!" Lavinia squealed as Nigel helped her out of the carriage. "It *is* made of sod!"

"Kansas brick, they call it," said Sir Roger with a chuckle.

"How barbaric!" she cried. "Why don't they just use wood?"

I felt my face get hot. My house had flaws, but I was proud of it. The walls were two feet thick at the bottom and fourteen inches at the top. I had helped Pa measure. The house was cool in the summer and warm in the winter, or at least coolish and warmish. And Pa had built the whole thing for exactly ten dollars and five cents, and that was for the few pieces of lumber in the house.

"Do you see any trees around here, Lavinia?" Nigel said. I was glad to hear a bit of impatience in his voice. "Wood is like gold in these parts."

He was right. Since wood and coal were precious, we burned buffalo chips whenever we could find them, "chips" being a more refined term for dried-up chunks of buffalo dung. But I didn't mention this to Lavinia.

"Cabby!" said a delighted voice. Emmeline rushed around the corner of the house, a flour-sack apron over her dress and her hair tied up in a rag. It must have been soap-making day—I could smell the foul smell from the outdoor kettle.

"Oh!" she gasped, taking in Nigel and Lavinia and the Banisters.

"How quaint you look," Lavinia cried, not waiting to be introduced. "So very rustic."

Poor Emmeline. She put her hand to the rag on her head, and her eyes flew from Lavinia's feather-trimmed bonnet to the dainty white-gloved hand resting on Nigel's arm. I knew what she was thinking: this was Lady Ashford, Nigel's *wife*.

Ma came out of the house, her face tense and anxious. "Mr. Ashford? Won't you . . . come inside?" She didn't even look at me. I couldn't figure what was wrong.

Once everyone had squeezed through the doorway and stood crowded together inside, Nigel introduced himself and his guests. "Sir Roger and Lady Margaret Banister, and Miss Lavinia Peacock."

Emmeline looked from Lavinia to Nigel. "*Lady* Ashford is . . .?"

"The journey would be too much for my mother, I'm afraid," Nigel said.

"Your mother! . . . I'm sorry," Emmeline murmured. But her eyes sparkled, and the dimple appeared in her cheek. She knew now: Nigel Ashford wasn't married after all.

"I regret my husband is off working in the north field," Ma said in a strained voice. "Is Cabby . . . is my daughter comporting herself adequately?"

Now I knew what was wrong with her. She thought I was a failure as a housemaid and Nigel had come here to return me. Didn't that just figure. Here I was, trying to solve my family's problems, and my mother only thought the worst of me.

"Fine, fine . . ." Nigel said absently. Before he could say more, Orin and Jesse burst inside.

"Look at these fine frontier lads!" Lavinia gushed. My brothers stood staring at her like she was an actual peacock who had flown through our door. How was I ever going to get Nigel and Emmeline together?

Chapter 15

"Do you want to see our milk cow?" Jesse said suddenly. He hadn't stopped staring at Lavinia. "Her name is Ulysses S. Grant."

Thank you, Jesse, this was just the chance I needed. "That's right, Miss Lavinia," I said as sweetly as I knew how. "Orin named her after the president, but we call her Lissie. *Do* come see her." I opened the door, and Lavinia swept out. "Sir Roger, Lady Banister?" I added, holding my breath. They followed Lavinia while Nigel remained behind. So far, so good.

The cow was picketed out past the well. Orin, Jesse, and I led our three guests to her, and I made sure to admire her from all sides. Fortunately, Lissie had filled out some since the terrible winter. Then I showed them the shed for the cow and horses, which was a flimsy thing made of sticks and hay. I showed them the chicken coop, which was just about the only thing made of wood at our place, and the chickens pecking around it. Then the cornfield, with the stalks standing straight and tall. There wasn't much to see, but I made the most of it all. Lavinia wanted genuine Kansas, and I showed it to her. Slowly.

When there was nothing left to show except the

necessary, which I figured I should skip, I ran back to the house ahead of the others and peeked through an open window. Ma, Emmeline, and Nigel sat around the table. I watched as Nigel took a big drink from a tin cup. "Aah," he said, "there's nothing like fresh, cold water on a hot day, I always say."

I had never heard him say that, actually.

"You're so right, Mr. Ashford," Emmeline replied, her eyes shining. She had pulled the rag off her head, and her hair tumbled around her shoulders. I thought she looked pretty.

"Call me Nigel, please," Nigel said. A very good sign. "Tell me, what do you do for pleasure around here, Emmeline?"

Uh-oh.

Emmeline looked doubtfully at Ma. Then she brightened. "The Fourth of July in Slocum City is most delightful. Everyone decorates their wagons with flags and bunting, and there's a parade, and fireworks—only the town can't afford them this year, because of the grasshoppers . . ."

"American Independence Day!" Nigel exclaimed. "So glad you mentioned it! I hope you'll come—"

At that exact moment, Lavinia burst through the door, followed by the Banisters. "My goodness!" Lavinia said, blinking her round blue eyes at Nigel, "what a ferocious-looking cow! Those long horns are simply terrifying!"

There she went, butting in again.

I followed Lavinia and the Banisters inside, and Lavinia prowled around the house, squeezing into the spaces between beds and bureaus, stove and table, poking her nose into everything. She picked up an edge of the rag rug. "A dirt floor. Imagine that!"

"Everything must get frightfully soiled," Lady Banister said with a shudder. She sat on the very edge of a wooden chair, trying not to touch anything.

She was right, actually. Our house was dark and dirty. I thought about explaining that Pa was going to buy lumber and build us a real house, except that the grasshoppers came. But I didn't say it. The way Lavinia and the Banisters talked, the way they inspected our private things, it was like we weren't even there. Ma's mouth hardened into a line, and Orin put his arm across Jesse's shoulders, staring indignantly at Lavinia. Suddenly, all I wanted was to get these people out of my house.

"I wonder what happens when it rains!" Lavinia said.

"These walls must be crawling with bugs," Lady Banister said, shuddering again.

I had an idea. "You better believe it," I said, turning to Lavinia. "Some of the centipedes are six inches long."

"Really?" Lavinia squeaked, glancing at the floor. Lady Banister drew up her skirt in alarm.

"Don't worry," I said. "Usually the snakes eat the centipedes."

I stole a peek at Ma, but, surprisingly, she didn't look mad. "Sometimes at night the snakes drop right out of the ceiling," I went on.

This had happened once—it was a perfectly harmless snake—so technically I was exaggerating, not lying.

"You have to keep your eyes open," Orin chimed in, "so they don't drop down your back."

Lavinia yelped. Everybody, even Nigel, looked at the ceiling.

"Children," Ma murmured, but she shot me a glance, the corners of her mouth twitching. For a second, I felt a cord of understanding run between us.

Lavinia put her hands to her neck, holding her dress closed. "Nigel, shouldn't we be going? I . . . I think it's getting dark."

"Oh, must you go?" Emmeline said. She looked so upset that I felt a pang of regret. Had my big mouth messed things up? Had I slowed the progress of true love?

"I'm afraid so," Nigel said. He bowed to Ma. "Thank you for your hospitality." He and Sir Roger went for the horses, and Emmeline brought the ladies their shawls and parasols, which Ma had piled on her bed.

"Come here, Cabby," Ma said as everyone bustled about. "You're behaving yourself at Ashford Manor?" The smile was gone.

In my mind I heard Mrs. Shaw scolding, saw a teapot smashing on the ground, saw myself sliding guiltily from a borrowed pony. "Yes, Ma," I muttered. The cord of understanding was broken.

"Pa had to pay for some repairs on the plow," Ma said. "Did you bring your wages?"

Of course I didn't bring my wages. I should have earned six dollars by now, but instead I owed the Ashfords another thirty cents. "Not this time, Ma," I whispered, my head hanging. I couldn't bring myself to explain.

Nigel stuck his head through the doorway. "Ready, ladies?"

"Oh, yes!" Lavinia cried. She had lost her enthusiasm for genuine sod houses, it seemed.

Emmeline looked like she wanted to cry, but just then Nigel stepped back inside, smiling at her. "As I started to say earlier, there's to be a horse race in Slocum City on Independence Day. I'm riding my thoroughbred, Admiral. Won't you come and wish me luck?"

My sister's face lit up with happiness. "Of course I will!"

Nigel bowed. "Until the Fourth, then."

Emmeline swayed. I think she almost fainted.

"Go on, Cabby," Ma said.

"Cabby has to go back?" Jesse said, and I felt like bawling. Instead, I hugged him and Orin and Emmeline, hustled out the door, and climbed onto my perch behind the carriage. The carriage jiggled as Nigel climbed onto his seat at the front, and we started rolling. "Say hi to Pa!" I called to my brothers and sister in the doorway, a huge lump in my throat. If only I *didn't* have to go back.

But at least Nigel wanted Emmeline to cheer for him in the horse race. That meant something, I was sure. Maybe my brilliant inspiration would work out after all, and they would get married. My sister would have a fairy tale come true, and the Potts family would have the money they needed, courtesy of Nigel Ashford. A triumph of true love *and* arithmetic.

As I watched my claim roll away, it wasn't hard to imagine acres of prairie replaced by fields of corn. And wheat. I had learned from Mr. Rouse that wheat was well suited to Kansas. Since I was daydreaming, I added a good-sized herd of cows—Angus cattle, like Nigel's—and a windmill turning busily beside the house to provide us with water.

Just a little money to get us through the rough patch, that's all we needed. Like Ma said, our house was small, but the land was big.

It was going to happen. Keep hoping, keep hoping, said the wheels of the carriage as my home faded in the distance.

Chapter 16

The next day was the twenty-seventh of June. Only one week 'til the Fourth of July. Unbelievably, Mrs. Shaw said I could take the holiday off. "I suppose the whole 'ousehold will go to Slocum City. Even Milady. She scolded the Master for buying that 'orse of his, but she won't pass up a race."

"I 'ope Nigel don't break 'is neck while Milady's watching," Mr. Shaw said. You could generally count on him to see the dark side of things.

"Fiddlesticks, Mr. Shaw," said Mrs. Shaw. "Mr. Ashford will be just fine."

To make sure Mrs. Shaw didn't change her mind about my day off, I threw myself into housemaiding with gusto. On Tuesday I starched and ironed fourteen shirts and eleven pocket handkerchiefs without burning a single one. On Wednesday I got through the day without mixing up my brushes or putting a spoon where a fork should be. On Thursday I wiped the soot off Ashford Manor's twenty-nine oil lamps and trimmed all twenty-nine wicks to the perfect angle. "Hmmp, not bad," Mrs. Shaw said.

On Friday I got paid for the first time. It wasn't much, just one dollar and seventy cents for all the time I'd been at Ashford Manor, but it felt good to have money in my pocket.

After giving me my pay, Mrs. Shaw sent me to the garden, a job I enjoyed even in the broiling Kansas heat. I set down my basket and pulled radishes from the dirt, their tops wilted and parched. The sun blasted the back of my neck, and I wished I had a sunbonnet. Housemaid caps weren't too practical for outdoor work.

Eli leaned over the wall. "Hey, Cabby. Seen your rattler friend?"

"Nope," I said, squinting up at him. "You going to the horse race on the Fourth of July?" It was almost natural now, talking to Eli.

"Of course I'm going. Mr. Rouse is riding Three-Legs." Eli looked as proud as a cat with a good-sized mouse, and I remembered that Three-Legs came from Mrs. Lewis's livery stable.

"That's nice. But . . ." I considered how to put this tactfully. "Isn't Three-Legs a little short, I mean compared to Admiral and all?"

"So what! He's got smarts and loads of heart."

"I know he does," I said, remembering the pony's pricked ears and eager way. "I hope he wins! Or . . . comes in second, after Admiral."

"Admiral? That monster?"

I smiled. "I have my reasons, actually."

"Which are?"

Should I tell him? Well, why not? I stood up and wiped my hands on my apron. "Ni—Mr. Ashford—particularly asked *my sister* to root for him and Admiral."

Eli looked blank.

"And . . . one could assume . . . I mean it's probably obvious . . ." This was difficult, for some reason. "I think Mr. Ashford is fond of my sister."

"Huh," Eli said, scratching his hair under his cap. "What about that frilly girl he was always with? Miss Rooster, or something like that."

"Oh, Lavinia Peacock," I said airily. "She's gone back to England. Mr. Ashford doesn't like her at all."

"Huh," Eli said again.

"What, you don't think Mr. Ashford could fall in l—be fond of my sister? Just because she's not Lady Watkins Winkleworth, or whatever?"

"That's not it," Eli said. "Or not all of it." He took a breath. "I actually really like your sister. She always talks to Ma at the post office. She and Mr. Meacham are the only ones who do."

I felt a prick of guilt. I had certainly never talked to Eli's ma at the post office. When she picked up her mail, Mrs. Lewis kept her head down, a shawl almost covering her face. The other customers stood back like there was an invisible fence around her. But Emmeline always smiled at Mrs. Lewis. She'd say things like, "Windy today, isn't it? I got blown to pieces this morning." If Mrs. Lewis didn't answer, she'd smile all the more.

"What are you saying, Eli Lewis? What's your point?" If he was trying to say that Emmeline was the nicest girl in Kansas, I already knew it.

Before he could answer, Mr. Rouse strolled up. "Hey there, young-uns."

"Hey, Mr. Rouse," we both said.

Mr. Rouse took off his hat, wiped his bald head with a

bandana, and chuckled. "You know this boy's an Indian, don't you, Cabby? You better hang on to that yellowy scalp of yours."

Eli went as still as the stones he leaned on.

I felt the blood pound in my head. "Mr. Rouse . . ."

Mr. Rouse roared with laughter. "You kids know I'm only joking. Why, me and Eli are the best of pals." He strolled off, still laughing.

The farm manager's ugly words hung in the air like a bad smell. Eli's shoulders sagged, and he stared at the ground.

"I'm sorry," I said in a tiny voice. "I mean it, I'm really sorry."

Eli shrugged. He didn't meet my eyes. "It doesn't matter, Cabby."

But it did matter.

Some jokes, even from a "pal," were more like a punch in the gut.

The night before the Fourth of July, at about nine in the evening, Nigel strolled into the kitchen while Mrs. Shaw and I were finishing up. "Almost forgot to mention it, Mrs. Shaw," he said, "but I've asked a few people over after the race tomorrow."

Mrs. Shaw stared at Nigel. I did too.

"Just Edwin Dumphrey, if he can stand it after I beat him"—Nigel laughed—"and the Banisters, of course, and the Thistlewaites and Rupert Spencer, and perhaps one or two more."

"But Mr. Ashford," Mrs. Shaw said, "it's a 'oliday, sir. I've already given the girl off, and Mr. Shaw and meself were . . ."

I held my breath. I already had my best dress, brooch pinned to the collar, laid out on my bed for the morning.

"Oh, it needn't be much," Nigel said. "Perhaps veal pies, and ox tongue, and sandwiches, that sort of thing. Some strawberry tarts, of course."

Without wanting to, I replayed my conversation with Eli in my mind. "I actually really like your sister," he had said. Was he hinting that Nigel wasn't nice enough for the nicest girl in Kansas? Was he right, possibly? Was Nigel being selfish?

Stop it, Cabby, I instructed myself. Nigel wasn't selfish, he was . . . the son of a Lord. Sons of Lords didn't take housemaids' holiday plans into account, and that's just the way it was.

Nigel breezed out of the kitchen, and Mrs. Shaw thumped heavily into a chair. I couldn't bring myself to look at her. If she canceled my day off . . .

"Well, lass, you'll get up and 'elp me before you leave?" she said finally.

"Yes, Ma'am, I will!" My spirits soared like a bird—but sank again when I saw how downcast Mrs. Shaw looked. I got the day off, and she didn't.

"That's a good girl," she sighed. "Mr. Shaw says it's going to rain tomorrow anyway. A 'oliday's no fun in the rain."

I glanced out the window. The sky was clear, fading from blue to black. It wasn't going to rain. Mr. Shaw always made gloomy predictions that didn't come true. But I was beginning to understand why. If you expected the worst, you couldn't be disappointed when your employers knocked your plans to bits.

"Have you worked for the Ashfords long?" I asked. It was easier to be bold in the half-dark kitchen.

"I should say so!" Mrs. Shaw said. "I started as a scullery maid, about your age."

How many years ago was that? Mrs. Shaw was older than Ma, for sure . . .

"Mr. Shaw was a hall boy," Mrs. Shaw went on. "Blacked the boots and lugged the coal and such. We've both been with the Ashfords ever since."

Her whole life, almost. Mrs. Shaw had been a servant her whole life.

"Except when my children were babies," she added. "I took some time off then."

"You have children?" This had never occurred to me.

"Naturally. Two gals, Eliza and Nancy, and a boy, Bertie. All grown now."

"Do you miss them? Is it hard, being a . . ." I couldn't say that word, *servant*.

There was a silence in the dim kitchen. "Sure, I miss them, and it *is* 'ard sometimes. But I was a village lass with no prospects." Mrs. Shaw's voice thickened. "Don't *you* be a servant your whole life, missy, not if you can 'elp it."

A lump rose in my throat. "I won't." I had never meant a promise more sincerely in my life.

I went over and kissed Mrs. Shaw's broad cheek.

"Pshaw," she said, but I think she was pleased.

Chapter 17

Next morning, I was up before the sun, whipping eggs so energetically they foamed over the side of the bowl.

"Slow down, there, Cabby," Mrs. Shaw said with a yawn.

I tried to slow down, but I felt like sparks ran through my fingers. "Did you hear that?" I cried. "That thump—listen, there's another one! That's the towns shooting off their cannons for the Fourth of July. Slocum City doesn't actually have a cannon, but Mr. Sawyer, he's the blacksmith, puts a mess of gunpowder on his anvil and explodes it. You can hear it from—"

"You're babbling, child," Mr. Shaw said. "Over-excitement's bound to make you sick."

Of course I was excited. A holiday and a horse race! And one more step in my marriage project.

I wished I could fly like a hawk straight to Slocum City. But an hour later, I sat in the buggy, wild with impatience, while Eli drove. *Plop, plop, plop,* went Georgiana's hooves. "Can't you hurry this stupid horse up?" I said for maybe the hundredth time. "We're going to miss the race."

"We are *not* going to miss the race. It's not 'til one o'clock." For some reason, there was a scowl as thick as oatmeal on Eli's face.

When we finally got to Mrs. Lewis's livery stable outside town, I was surprised to see the yard full of sleek, long-legged thoroughbreds—and one black-and-white pony, my friend Three-Legs. "Ma's boarding the horses for the race," Eli explained.

"That's nice," I said, hopping down and blowing Three-Legs a kiss. "C'mon, Eli, let's go!" Strains of "Yankee Doodle" floated toward us from the center of town.

"You go on," Eli muttered. "I'll come later."

"Why? You need to help your ma with the horses?"

"I *said,* you go on. I'll be there for the race."

Something was the matter with Eli. Whatever it was, he certainly lacked holiday spirit.

But I wasn't going to let Eli Lewis spoil my day. I jumped down and hurried the quarter-mile to town, marching in time to the music.

Fourth of July was the one day a year Slocum City got gussied up. Red, white, and blue bunting hung every- where; flags fluttered from posts and doorways and even on horses' bridles. Everybody wore their Sunday best, and ladies had traded sunbonnets for their fanciest hats. The music came from a raised stage near the train depot, where the men who owned any kind of instrument blew into them or scraped away as hard as they could.

Everything was like it always was on Independence Day, except for the Prince Albert folks mixed into the crowd. They stood out like lilies in a field of Kansas sunflowers, the men in linen jackets and the ladies in their summer dresses gathered into fashionable bustles.

I hurried through the crowd, looking for my family and saying hi to everyone. I waved to the Buchanans, who were doing a good business selling lemonade outside the Grand Paris. A big block of ice sweated in its burlap wrapper in a tub beside them.

"Hey!" I called to Bub Skyler, who had actually changed out of his overalls for the occasion.

"You ain't drowned yourself in one of them gold-plated bathtubs, I see!" he crowed, clapping me on the shoulder.

I grinned. "Not yet."

"Hi, Mr. Meacham!" I called to Knee-High. He was on the stage, perched on a folding chair that looked tiny beneath him.

"G-good to see you, C-Cabby!" He mopped his whiskery face before picking up his trumpet and starting in on "Yankee Doodle" again. Slocum City's band didn't know many tunes.

I didn't notice our closest neighbors the Nybergs until Mr. Nyberg touched my arm. "Cabby Potts! Iss dat you?"

"Hey, Mr. Nyberg." I waved to Mrs. Nyberg and the little kids hiding behind her skirt, their hair so blond it looked white. I could never remember which kid was which.

"How plump you look," Mrs. Nyberg said. "Like a peach." She pinched my cheek to prove it. "They feed you well, no?"

How could I explain? Yes, the Ashfords fed me well—as long as I didn't try to eat with them.

"Yes, I mean, thanks. You look good, too." But that was a lie. Mr. and Mrs. Nyberg looked stringy and ragged. The kids were hollow-eyed. Their cow had died during the winter, I remembered, and Ma gave them a couple of her chickens.

"Your family iss over dere," Mrs. Nyberg said, pointing.

"Thanks—happy Fourth of July," I said, but I wasn't quite as excited as before. The grasshoppers had left their mark on this town, maybe on the Nybergs most of all. At Ashford Manor, it was easy to forget that.

I hurried toward my family, pushing the Nybergs out of my mind. Ma was wearing her best calico dress and pearl hair combs. Emmeline wore Ma's old blue-silk hoop dress, only slightly chewed by the grasshoppers. Her chestnut hair was pinned up in a sort of swirl, with Ma's black velvet hat perched on top. My sister looked fancy, if a bit mountainous on the bottom half. I saw one of the Prince Albert ladies point at the hoop skirt and titter at the old-fashioned style. Hopefully Emmeline didn't notice.

"My little Cabbage!" Pa exclaimed when I ran up. "We didn't know you were coming!" He folded me into a hug, and I breathed in the smell of pipe smoke and good Kansas dirt on his Sunday suit. Ma pecked me on the cheek.

"Here, Ma, I brought my wages," I said, handing her the money from my pocket.

Ma smiled. When her face relaxed you could tell how much she looked like Emmeline, only with the shine sort of rubbed off. Then her face hardened. "Where's the rest of the money, Cabby? You haven't gone and spent it on some foolish thing?"

I should have warned her it wasn't as much as she expected. Still, how could she think I would fritter away my pay? They were *my* earnings, but I had never considered keeping them for myself. I felt like she had slapped me.

"Now, Martha . . ." Pa began.

"I had a . . . an accident," I managed to say. "I had to pay for some things."

"Oh, Cabby," Ma breathed, and the disappointment was worse than the anger.

I felt a little better once I was strolling with Emmeline through the holiday crowd, trying not to step on the wire hoops of her dress. She wanted to know everything, so I told her about breaking the china, and the rattlesnake, and Lady Ashford finally calling me by name, and Mr. Shaw being gloomy all the time, and maybe learning to iron. The only thing I didn't mention, for some reason, was Eli Lewis.

My sister listened to all of it, throwing in "poor Cabby!" or "my goodness!" at the exact right times. It smoothed out the rough places in my heart, like butter on brown bread.

I wanted to know everything too, so she told me about Dr. Wattles' pigs escaping into the street, and Mrs. Snopes having a conniption when the visiting preacher was a Baptist instead of a Methodist. "*And* . . . can you keep a secret?"

"Sure."

"You know all those letters Bub Skyler's been getting?

Turns out they're from a *lady* back East. Bub put an advertisement in a magazine, and she answered it."

"No!"

"Isn't that romantic? Bub said she's coming soon . . ."

All at once, Nigel Ashford appeared in front of us, and Emmeline stopped talking as if she'd been struck dumb. Nigel wore sleek striped trousers tucked into black boots, and carried his riding whip in his hand. The waxed ends of his moustache curved up like a second smile. Even I thought he looked handsome. The Ladyship was with him, dressed in a gray silk dress positively drenched with pearls. Jewels glinted on her fingers adorned her white hair. Next to her, Emmeline looked like she was dressed for milking.

"Well, just who I was hoping to see!" Nigel exclaimed, bowing to us. "My mother wants to see the town before the race." He laughed like this was a funny idea. "Perhaps you could . . ."

Emmeline opened her mouth but nothing came out.

"Sure, we can show you around," I said quickly. Here was my second opportunity to bring Nigel and my sister together, and I wouldn't let it pass by.

Chapter 18

"Come on," I whispered to my sister, tugging her along. Emmeline, Nigel, the Ladyship, and I started up the street, probably the strangest foursome in Slocum City's history. "That's the land office where Mr. H. H. Mortimer works," I said, the words tumbling out any which way. "You go there if you want to file a claim. And next door is Smitty's Saloon and Cigar Shop, which I guess you can tell from the sign—I've never actually been inside—and next to that is Prouty's Boarding House, or it used to be before it closed because of the grasshoppers, now it's not anything. And there's Mr. Snopes's Barber Shop and Shave Palace, and the grocery, and here is Knee-High's, I mean Mr. Meacham's store—that's him up there, with the trumpet."

"Very interesting," Lady Ashford said faintly. I thought she looked pale, and she leaned heavily on her cane.

Before I could start again, Mr. Hanley, who was both the mayor and banker of Slocum City, stepped onto the stage. He was a stooped, unhappy sort of person, maybe because so few people put money into his bank. "Ladies and gentlemen, the 'Star Spangled Banner'?" he called, like he was sorry to interrupt everybody.

The band played a few notes, and people crowded

around. "What's happening?" Lady Ashford asked. Someone spit tobacco juice dangerously close to her silk skirt.

"It's their national anthem, Mother," Nigel replied. Emmeline gazed at him like he'd said something profound. She still hadn't uttered a word, but her eyes were shining and her cheeks glowed pink.

Everyone sang, then the band got down and Mr. H. H. Mortimer got up, dressed as always in his black bow tie, his hair so shiny it looked wet, his long sideburns trimmed into mutton chops. He started off, like he always did, with the "sweet milk of liberty" and "never shall the tyrant's fist," that sort of thing. Oh dear, he could go on for ages. I looked around for a way to escape, but we were packed in pretty tight.

Suddenly Lady Ashford grasped my arm. "Sophie— get Sophie," she commanded weakly.

"Uh, Sophie isn't . . . she isn't here." In fact, I had seen that useless woman on the bench outside Smitty's Saloon, nodding off already. I didn't know what to do.

Just then someone very tall stepped up. "Does the l-lady n-n-need to get out of the s-sun?"

"Yes, thank you, Mr. Meacham!" Emmeline said.

"Wouldn't want to impose," Nigel said, but Knee-High ignored him and led us toward his shop. He was so big, he parted the crowd like a cow catcher on a train. When he opened the door, his white cat shot out, turned to hiss at Emmeline, and slipped away.

Knee-High led us into the half-dark store and found a chair for Lady Ashford. "C-cooler here than upstairs." The Ladyship sank into the chair, her hand to her chest.

If she was bothered by the pots and pans hanging over her head, she didn't show it. Her face looked as gray as her dress.

While Nigel paced around the store, tapping his whip on his boot tops, Emmeline knelt beside Lady Ashford's chair, her hoop skirt billowing around her. The Ladyship pulled a handkerchief from her sleeve and coughed so deep and hard it seemed she would never get a breath. I looked away. This kind of thing gave me the scaredy-scares, as Orin used to say.

"Come here, Cabby," Emmeline said.

I stepped closer, reluctantly.

"She needs more air. Help me unbutton her dress."

What? No, I couldn't do it. "I-I'll go find Ma."

"You'll do no such thing, Catherine Potts," Emmeline said. It was strange how my sister could turn all business when she needed to. I'd seen her sob over a rabbit caught in a trap and then twist the creature's neck with a steady hand.

The next thing I knew, she had shooed Nigel and Knee-High out of the store and we both knelt beside Lady Ashford, unfastening what seemed like hundreds of silk-covered buttons. Fortunately, they went up the *back* of her dress.

"What's the matter with her?" Emmeline whispered, fingers flying.

"Consumption," I whispered back.

"Oh, poor thing. Now the corset, Cabby."

Fortunately, Lady Ashford's coughing eased when her corset was looser. She sank against the back of the chair. The handkerchief in her hand, I saw with a wrench of my stomach, was flecked with blood. "Something to drink," she said in a hoarse whisper.

Whew. If she could give orders, she was feeling better.

"Of course," Emmeline said. She fished in her pocket and handed me a nickel. "Go buy her some lemonade."

I grabbed a tin feed scoop—in the jumble of Knee-High's goods, this was the closest I could find to a cup—and ran outside, passing between Nigel and Knee-High on either side of the doorway. It was a relief to be outside.

When I got back, only Knee-High was standing guard at the door. I pushed the door part way open, the scoop in my hand, then stopped, amazed.

Lady Ashford was asleep in the chair, her head tipped back against a cast-iron kettle hanging on a post. My sister and Nigel stood beside her, so deep in quiet conversation they didn't even notice me. I could tell how easy and natural it was, just talking to each other. Nigel said something and Emmeline laughed quietly. She said something back, and he put his hand on her arm. Then he leaned down and kissed her, right on the lips.

Chapter 19

I gulped. A big part of me did not like seeing my own sister get kissed. I took a step out of the store—and ran right into Knee-High. Lemonade sloshed out of the scoop and onto his trousers. "Sorry," I said. Had he seen what I saw? This was all so embarrassing.

Knee-High's face was blank, but his big hands clenched into fists. "Is L-L-lady A-A-A . . .?" He shook his head like he was trying to jar the words loose.

"Lady Ashford's sleeping," I said. Knee-High nodded and strode off.

I stood on the sidewalk, my hands shaking, trying not to spill the rest of the lemonade. As my embarrassment faded, I started to see the good side of the situation. People didn't go around kissing other people for no reason, right? In fact, the only reason I knew of was true love. Somehow, my brilliant inspiration had just inched closer to reality.

A few minutes later, Nigel, Emmeline, and the Ladyship emerged from the store, Lady Ashford leaning on Nigel's arm. Someone in the street called, "Hullo, Ash. I've been looking for you, chap." It was a ruddy-faced young man wearing tight trousers and riding boots like Nigel's.

"Hullo there, Edwin," Nigel said, settling Lady Ashford on the bench. I handed her the scoop of lemonade, and she sipped slowly. "This is my mother, Lady Ashford," Nigel told Edwin.

And? And? What about Emmeline? And me?

"Mother, this is Edwin Dumphrey, recently arrived from London," Nigel said, as the young man bowed to Lady Ashford.

"Edwin . . . Son of Lord Dumphrey, Viscount of Danderbridge?" Lady Ashford asked, her voice firmer now.

"That's right, your Ladyship. *Third* son," Edwin added, twisting up his mouth like he'd eaten something bitter. He turned to Nigel. "You do remember we have a race to run? Our mounts await."

"Indeed," Nigel said, stepping into the street. "Mother—I must go." He turned around, tipped his hat in the general direction of Emmeline and me, and hurried off with Edwin.

I flushed hot with fury. But before I could say anything to my sister, Sophie waddled up. "Ooh, Madame, I look for you *partout,*" she panted. That little hypocrite. She helped Lady Ashford up, and they walked slowly across the street.

I didn't dare look at Emmeline. I could only imagine what she was feeling. Not that I knew how gentlemen were supposed to behave right after kissing someone, but not like nothing at all had happened.

Amazingly, she took my hand, her eyes alight with happiness. "Cabby, I'm in love. I am absolutely in love."

"Uh, that's nice."

"It was like we'd known each other *forever.* He told me

about his dogs and horses back in England . . ."

That didn't sound very romantic, but okay.

". . . and how his mother got sick, and I said how sorry I was, and he thanked me for taking care of her, then he . . . he ki—"

"You can skip the details," I said quickly. Actually, I was curious. What did it feel like? Was it pleasant? But I couldn't bring myself to talk about kissing. "Did he ask you to marry him?" I asked instead.

Emmeline dropped my hand. "Of course not! I mean . . . not yet . . . I mean, Cabby Potts, you don't know how love works!"

"I never said I did. I was just asking a question."

"Besides, we'll have to keep things secret, at least for a while."

"Did he say that?" I demanded. "In those words?"

"No-o-o, not in those words, exactly, but it's obvious, isn't it? Why else would he not introduce me to his friend? Isn't it romantic?" Emmeline murmured. "It's like Romeo and Juliet. A forbidden love."

"I guess." Now that she put it that way, it sort of made sense. Nigel couldn't go around announcing his love for a Kansas sod-buster's daughter, especially in front of his mother. He'd have to warm the Ladyship up to the idea more gradually, I supposed.

No, Nigel wasn't being rude when he acted like nothing had happened. He was being careful, cautious, *surreptitious.* Right?

"Clear the street! Clear the street!" a man with a bull-horn yelled. "The race is about to begin."

I ran into the store and returned Knee-High's feed scoop, then Emmeline and I hurried across the street. We found Ma and Pa and the boys in the crowd on the railroad platform. We had just gotten settled when Orin yelled, "Here they come!"

"Here they come!" echoed other voices as a half-dozen Prince Albert gentlemen led their horses toward a line painted on the street just beyond Knee-High's store. The English thoroughbreds were beautiful, with arched necks and polished flanks and sideways, skittish prancing. Edwin Dumphrey led a sleek bay horse, but the biggest and most beautiful was coal-black Admiral, strutting like he knew he was the star of the show. I heard *ooh*'s from the crowd, then murmurs as the stallion flattened his ears and kicked out at a horse behind him.

"That horse looks dangerous," Emmeline breathed in my ear. "What if Nigel gets hurt? I couldn't bear it."

"He'll be fine," I said, already a little tired of Emmeline-in-love. But even I felt a nervous prickle.

"Look at the pipsqueak!" someone yelled, and a few people laughed. Here came Three-Legs, led by his rider Mr. Rouse, trotting to catch up with other horses. Three-Legs did look tiny next to them, but I didn't like folks laughing. He was the only Kansas horse in the race.

Which reminded me: where was Eli Lewis?

"The race will be one mile," called the man with the bullhorn. "It will commence and end at the starting line. Today's contestants are . . ." While he talked, I scanned the crowd and finally spotted Eli standing by himself near the tracks, his felt cap pulled low on his forehead.

"Be back later," I said to Emmeline. I slipped over to

Eli. "Where have you been hiding?"

"I wasn't hiding!" he snapped.

"What's the matter, you grouch? Don't you like the Fourth of July?" I tried to remember if I'd ever seen Eli or his ma in town on the Fourth of July. I never had, I decided.

Eli shrugged. "It's fine, I guess. Are you going to watch the race or keep on blabbing?"

Before I could think of a suitable answer, the bullhorn man yelled, "Riders up!" Mr. Rouse hopped onto Three-Legs's back. A boy darted out with a wooden block, and one by one the other men swung themselves onto their horses. Even Nigel looked small on his long-legged mount.

"To the start!" yelled the man. The horses formed a line that stretched across the street, Three-Legs standing calmly while the thoroughbreds pranced.

My heart beat like a kettledrum. I could barely breathe. The bullhorn man clanged a giant cowbell, and the horses leaped away, thundering down Main Street. "And they're off!"

Chapter 20

The horses swept past. With all the dust, I had no idea who was in the lead. But it was obvious who was in the rear: Three-Legs, his three white legs and one black pumping furiously.

"Go, Three-Legs! Run!" I shrieked. "You too, Admiral!" I was so excited I almost grabbed Eli's hand but caught myself just in time.

When they reached the end of the street, the horses curved around behind the row of buildings and swept out of view. I heard the rumble of hooves and scattered yells and cheers from people along the course out on the prairie. The crowd around me buzzed, and some people slipped money from hand to hand. Hopefully Mrs. Snopes wouldn't see that. I could only imagine what she'd say about gambling.

A few minutes later, everyone cheered as the horses reappeared at the top of the street. "What's happening? Who's winning?" I yelled.

"Can't tell," Eli yelled back. "Wait—I think it's Admiral!"

The horses galloped toward the finish line. Yes, it was definitely Admiral in the lead, Nigel crouching over his neck. Behind him, a few lengths back, three more thoroughbreds raced neck and neck, Edwin Dumphrey's bay in the middle. It was thrilling how their manes and tails flew, their legs flashing almost in unison.

Suddenly the two horses on the outside veered toward Edwin's horse. All three horses, caught in a tangle, slowed down. Three-Legs swerved nimbly around the pack and shot ahead of them. "Hurray!" I screamed. I thought I might burst with happiness. Admiral would win, and my little Three-Legs would come in second.

The next instant, a white shape leaped off the roof of Nehemiah Meacham's General Store and Post Office, landing on the hitching rail in front of the store. It was Moonbeam, Knee-High's cat. That ornery feline, back arched and fur on end, stood on the rail and hissed at the horses thundering its way.

Admiral turned his head toward the cat, stopped short, and reared onto his hind legs. Nigel slid off the horse's back, landed in the dirt, and scrambled to the sidewalk. Meanwhile Three-Legs caught up to Admiral, the cat jumped off the rail, and the spotted pony galloped across the finish line. Three-Legs had won the race! Too bad about Admiral, but the little guy had done it.

Eli grinned at me, and I grinned back. I didn't hug him, because Potts girls did not hug boys in the middle of Main Street. But I wanted to.

As the rest of the horses swept across the line, some people yelled, "Hurray for the pipsqueak!" but others booed. "I lost seventy-five cents on that big English baby!" "Scared of a little ol' kitty cat."

Then, "Look! He's going crazy!" a farmer near me shouted. Admiral, stirrups swinging from his empty saddle, plunged and bucked in the street like he was possessed by demons. Nigel—at a safe distance from the flying hooves—waved his arms and yelled at his horse, which did no good at all.

"Grab him, Nigel!" bellowed one of the Prince Albert men. Nigel made a lunge for the reins, but Admiral twisted away, crashing into the boards of the sidewalk and sending a hind leg right through the window of Mr. Snopes's Barber Shop and Shave Palace. Splinters of wood and shards of glass flew everywhere.

"That beast is going to kill someone!" a woman screamed.

My blood running cold, I turned to Eli, but he was already racing across the street. He pushed past Nigel, ducked between Admiral's front hooves, and grabbed one dangling rein. The horse didn't calm down, though. He plunged and reared, his movements jerky, clumsy, desperate.

"Be careful, Eli!" I yelled.

"Look, something's wrong with the horse's leg!" Bub Skyler shouted.

I saw it now—one of Admiral's front legs was bent at an awful angle below the knee. It was pain that made the horse so crazy.

Just when it seemed Admiral would rip away from Eli, another shape darted in and grabbed the other rein. It was a woman with thick black braids hanging below her bonnet—Mrs. Lewis. Somehow, she and Eli managed to grasp Admiral's bridle and hold his head from both sides. The crowd hushed, holding its breath, and I could hear Mrs. Lewis saying something, right in the stallion's ear.

The words were Kiowa, I assumed. They were soothing but also commanding, kind of like Ma's when Jesse
got into the stinging ants. The horse quieted, his sides
heaving, flecks of foamy sweat dripping from his neck,
his proud head drooping almost to the ground.

I was so relieved my legs went all watery. But around
me I heard people muttering.

"What kind of heathen gibberish are you speaking to
that animal?" Mrs. Snopes called shrilly. She wormed her
way to the front of the crowd and pointed an accusing
finger at Eli's ma.

"She probably put some sort of spell on it," a man
said. "You can't trust an Indian."

"Half-Indian neither," said someone else. I think it
was Mrs. Hanley, the banker's wife.

Eli stared out at everyone, his face stony. Mrs. Lewis
turned her back to the crowd and stroked Admiral's
sweat-streaked neck.

I felt clobbered, the wind knocked out of me. How
had everything gone so wrong so fast?

"They were *helping,*" I managed to croak. A few heads
swung in my direction, curious eyes scrutinizing me. And
I lost my courage. I wanted to say more, wanted to stand
up for Eli and his ma, but it was like someone clamped a
hand over my mouth. Where was my intemperate tongue
when I needed it?

Mr. Rouse approached. With him was Knee-High
Meacham and old Dr. Wattles, Slocum City's only doctor.
Mr. Rouse took Admiral's reins, and Eli and Mrs. Lewis
slipped away.

Dr. Wattles was a people doctor, not a horse doctor,

but he leaned over and felt Admiral's leg with his finger-tips. Then he straightened up, shaking his head.

Mr. Rouse handed Nigel something. It was a silver pistol.

A terrible hush settled on the crowd. It seemed like that pistol sucked all the sound out of Main Street. Even the wind died down, and all the flags went still.

Knee-High clapped his hands for attention. "Almost t-time for baseball!" he called. "Slocum City's third annual game of b-baseball!" I thought he sounded awfully cheerful considering the circumstances. "Come on everybody, this way." He hardly stammered at all.

I found my family and walked with them. Just a minute later, a pistol shot rang out with a *crack*. I knew it was coming, but I still flinched.

"Is it fireworks, Pa?" Jesse asked.

"No, Jesse, it's not fireworks," Pa answered gently.

I realized then why Knee-High had shooed people along. I tried to catch his eye to thank him, but he stood in the middle of the street, staring at Emmeline, while people washed around him. His face looked so sad it made me want to cry. The next second he snapped out of it. "Everybody ready to p-play?" People's long faces brightened, and kids went scurrying for gloves, balls, and bats. In Slocum City, baseball was for girls *and* boys, maybe because there weren't enough boys.

I didn't play, but I stayed to watch the baseball game. It was Orin's first, and I knew he'd want me to. But my heart wasn't in it. I paced behind the rough wooden benches set up around a patch of scythed grass, my thoughts skipping to that dangling, crooked leg. And the pistol shot. And Eli and his ma standing there while people said cruel things.

No wonder Eli didn't like the Fourth of July. It was hard to celebrate America's birthday when folks didn't think of him as American. And more people in town meant more mouths to taunt him. It *wasn't* just jokes. It was ignorance and plain old prejudice.

In Kansas, folks were just folks. That was what I told myself back at Ashford Manor. But it wasn't true.

Orin got up to bat, face pale and intent, freckles standing out on his cheeks. Bub Skyler was pitching for the other team, and he wound up with his thick arm like he was going to throw the fastest pitch ever seen. Instead, he lobbed Orin a gentle floater.

Orin smacked the ball straight back at Bub. "Tarnation!" Bub yelled, letting the ball dribble between his feet. Orin raced to first base like a rabbit with a coyote on its heels. His team cheered loudly.

I smiled. Slocum City folks *were* good folks. They were my friends and neighbors. Why did they have to be so pig-headed?

Chapter 21

Ma spread a blanket on the ground, and I saw people fetching picnic baskets from their wagons. I wished I could stay, but I had promised to help Mrs. Shaw with Nigel's party. Not to mention that Ma might not have extra food for me. Based on last year's picnic, she'd have killed and fried exactly one chicken. Better to divide it by five than six.

I waved to Orin in the outfield and hugged Emmeline and Jesse, then Pa and even Ma. My feet heavy and my heart heavier, I walked out of town to the livery stable.

I found Eli hunched like a buzzard on the seat of the buggy, Georgiana already harnessed. "About time," he growled. I didn't defend myself. He had every reason to be in a bad mood.

"Why did they have to shoot Admiral?" I asked as we started for Ashford Manor. "Couldn't they patch up his broken leg?"

"Horses can't stand on three legs," Eli said. "And they can't stay lying down like people can. Admiral would have died anyway."

I pictured Admiral's flashing eyes and sleek black neck. "It's terrible."

"Yup."

"And it's a shame how people . . . how they . . ."

"Forget it," Eli said. "Me and Ma are used to it." But his face told a different story. Although he might be used to meanness, it bothered him plenty. Why hadn't I done more to defend him? What a coward I was.

We drove a ways, then Eli surprised me by stopping the buggy, Georgiana deciding to obey for once. "All this," he said, pointing with his chin across the prairie, "was tribal country. Kiowa, Cheyenne, Kansa, Wichita."

I said nothing. I hardly dared to look at him. If Eli was willing to let me into his family's history, I was ready to listen.

"When my ma was born, there were no towns or farms or railroads. The Kiowa followed the buffalo and lived off them. There was nothing more exciting than a buffalo hunt, according to Ma."

I had never seen a live buffalo, but I tried to imagine a herd of enormous hump-backed animals thundering across the prairie, men on horseback galloping after them.

"Then the white people moved in. People coming from the East started settlements, some of them illegal, and plowed up the grass the buffalo needed to eat. And they shot buffalo by the thousands, sometimes just for sport."

I thought of the buffalo head on Nigel's study wall and felt a little sick. "Didn't the government do anything to help?"

"Do anything?" Eli snorted. "*For* the tribes?"

I had always thought of government as a good thing. I mean, the government gave away land to homesteaders like us. And I'd thought of homesteads as good things too, turning the wild grasslands into farms. But I'd never considered things from the tribes' point of view.

I shook my head. Simple, sharp lines had turned gray and fuzzy. Last Fourth of July, my biggest problem was talking Ma into buying us lemonade. How had everything gotten so complicated?

"Another thing the white people brought," Eli went on, "was disease. When my ma was ten years old, half her band died of a sickness that got into the water. Her mother—my *ti-gui-day* who I never met—died, and both her brothers too."

"Oh, no," I breathed.

"Eventually, the government forced all the tribes to move to Indian Territory. My ma was lucky in a way, because she married my pa . . ."

"How did they meet?" I interrupted. This promised to be the kind of romantic story Emmeline would love. Not that *I* cared about romance, of course. I was just curious.

Eli shrugged. "My ma and my pa knew each other for a long time, since Pa's father bought horses and buffalo hides from Ma's father. I guess they just . . ."

"Fell in love?" I prompted, feeling my cheeks burn.

"Uh, yeah. After they got married, she could stay in Kansas since my pa was white."

"What . . . what happened to your father?" I asked softly. Somehow I knew he was ready to tell me.

Eli looked away. In the long pause, I heard the cry of a nighthawk. Georgiana stamped her foot and whinnied, maybe to remind us that it was getting dark. "My pa died when I was eleven," he finally said. "On my birthday, actually."

There was a world of hurt in that sentence. "I'm so sorry," I said, although I knew it wasn't enough.

"Pa fell off the roof of the stable," Eli went on, his voice thick and husky. "He was never right after that. Ma had to take care of him and run the stable too, until he died."

"Your ma's had it rough." I hesitated, then added, "But I'm glad she has you."

"I guess. But she wants me to speak Kiowa, and it doesn't come natural to me." Eli wrapped the ends of the reins around and around his fist. "Me and Ma wouldn't fit in down in Indian Territory, and here . . . You know how folks are."

"I don't care what they think—and I don't care if you're Kiowa, or half Kiowa, or whatever," I said, blushing.

"Gee. Thanks for the permission, Cabby."

Why did I always say the wrong thing? "That's not what I meant. I just . . . You're okay with me, Eli Lewis, except for being a boy."

Eli gave me his quick, sideways grin. "And I guess you're okay with me, except for being half idiot—and all girl."

I tossed my head, in fun this time. Eli shook the reins, and Georgiana broke into a trot, eager to get home. As we jounced along the path, a question occurred to me. "Was that your name?"

"What?"

"Your ma called you something, back on the day you picked me up. Was that your Kiowa name? *Mikimi* or something like that?"

Eli pulled back on the reins. "Whoa, Georgiana!" The horse neighed in protest, but she stopped.

"I've never told a white person my Kiowa name," Eli said.

"I won't tell." I whispered, even though there was no one else in sight, just miles of waving grasses, the night-hawk circling and swooping as it hunted, and the light fading from the dark-blue sky.

"My Kiowa name is *Kehimi*," he said. "It was a chief's name, and it means Prairie Dog. Ma said I had bright eyes like a little prairie dog."

"*Kehimi*," I repeated. "That's nice. I don't think *my* name means anything."

"Cabby stands for Cabbage," Eli said solemnly, guessing at my nickname's nickname, "which means Stinky Vegetable Girl."

"Hey!" I had always liked it when Pa called me Cabbage, a cabbage being a useful and practical vegetable—but, in truth, a bit stinky. I fished for a cutting reply, but Eli's sideways smile made a melting place in my heart, and all I could do was smile back.

"Let's go, Georgiana!" Eli said, and she shot off at a canter.

—*Part 4*—

A Mysterious Letter

Chapter 22

Mrs. Shaw was in a scolding mood when I finally slipped into the kitchen, but she wasn't mad at me, exactly. "See this food?" she huffed. "Mr. Ashford's gone and canceled 'is party, not that I blame 'im exactly, but now all this is wasted—and me and Mr. Shaw's day, too."

That was the closest I had heard her come to criticizing Nigel.

"I told you nothing good would come of that 'orse race," Mr. Shaw said. For once, one of his dark predictions had come true.

"You might as well eat, lass," Mrs. Shaw sighed.

I was starving, so I ate two ham-salad sandwiches, a big helping of veal pot pie, and three strawberry tarts. My family would have been bug-eyed at the food, but I would have traded it for one-sixth of a fried chicken at my own sod house. Gladly.

Lying in bed with a full belly that night, I stared out the window at a winking star, the events of the crazy day flitting through my mind. A lot of them were sad, terrible really. But one of them was nice: Eli telling me his story and his name. And Nigel kissing Emmeline, of course! That was weird, but promising. A big step in my matchmaking scheme.

Before too long, hopefully, there would be a wedding. That's what always happened after a kiss, at least in Emmeline's romantic stories. My sister would become Lady Mrs. Honorable Emmeline Ashford, or something like that. Nigel would give us lots of money, I'd go back home at last, and everything would be like it should be . . . except of course that Emmeline would be married and would have to live at . . .

"Wake up, Lazy-bones!" said Mrs. Shaw's voice. "You think every day's a 'oliday?"

Yipes. Morning already. I pulled on my ugly black dress and apron, stuffed my hair into my cap, and hurried downstairs to the kitchen. I was anxious to see Nigel. He'd be sad about his horse, naturally, but maybe he'd ask about my sister. I whistled as I set the breakfast table, plotting what I'd say to him: "Her social schedule is quite busy," maybe, since it was best he didn't take her for granted. "But she can be found at the post office on Tuesdays and Fridays . . ."

Lady Ashford hobbled into the dining room on Sophie's arm. "Is that *whistling* I hear?" she snapped. She looked tired, and somehow even thinner than yesterday, but her expression was as Ladyship-like as ever. If she was embarrassed about me unbuttoning her dress in Knee-High Meacham's store, she sure didn't show it.

"Um, no . . . yes. Sorry, Milady," I said, feeling just a mite indignant. It wasn't like I expected a grateful hug, but who cared if I was whistling?

Lady Ashford settled into a dining room chair. I set a boiled egg into her gold-rimmed egg cup and turned to get the teapot from the buffet.

"It appears I am in your debt once again, Catherine," the Ladyship said suddenly.

I jumped. Fortunately, I did *not* drop the teapot. "No, you aren't," I said. "I mean, you don't have to pay me back. It was Emmeline's nickel, anyway."

Lady Ashford swiveled to look at me. "Nickel?" she said wonderingly, like she didn't know this word.

"Five cents. For the lemonade." She still looked at me blankly, and a far corner of my brain realized I had misunderstood her. But I babbled on. "It's not a lot of money, really, although a nickel is one twentieth of a dollar, which I guess you knew already, and a dollar actually is a lot of money." The more Lady Ashford stared, the more I babbled. "You see, since the grasshoppers ate all our crops last year, and a lot of our clothes and stuff too, we didn't make any money at all, so we're even more inconvenienced than usual, and Pa says we might have to give up the claim, and that's why I'm working here, to make two dollars a week . . ."

I froze. Nigel had come into the dining room and was staring at me curiously. I couldn't believe I had blurted out the story of my family's problems. I mean, it had to come out eventually, but at the right time and in the right way—*after* he proposed to Emmeline. How much had he heard?

Lady Ashford, anyway, had heard it all. She gazed at me thoughtfully, her expression unreadable. I filled her teacup, willing my hand not to shake.

"A Mr. Dumphrey's come over," Mrs. Shaw said later that afternoon. "Mr. Ashford wants tea in the stable." She gave a huge sigh as she sliced leftover sandwiches for the tea tray. I guess she was still mad at Nigel for canceling her Fourth of July then calling off his party.

"I'll take the tray," I said. I went out quickly, before Mrs. Shaw remembered I was supposed to stay away from the horses.

In the stable, I set the tray on a bale of hay for Nigel and Edwin, who lounged between two horse stalls, then went out and looked for a place to listen. Yes, it was spying, but it was for a good cause.

There was a watering trough under a window. I climbed up and stood tip-toe on the edge of the trough, watching as Nigel dropped his head into his hands and mumbled something I couldn't hear. He was upset about Admiral, I guessed. Poor Nigel.

"How much did you lose?" Edwin asked.

"Hundreds," Nigel said into his hands. "I had the race in the bag, if it wasn't for that infernal cat."

My pity blew away like a pinch of dust. Hundreds? Of dollars? Wagered and lost on a stupid horse race?

"Hopefully Mother won't find out," Nigel went on. He kicked at the bale of hay, making the teacups rattle. "I wish she'd stop making trouble for me with Father, complaining about my 'extravagant ways.' Why should she begrudge me a little fun?"

Edwin groaned. "I just got a stern letter from *my* father: 'Son, I expect you to comport yourself properly, et cetera, et cetera, remember that you must earn your own living, et cetera, et cetera.' Does he know what it's like to live on these blasted plains?" He looked around like he was surveying the Kansas prairie, and I had to duck quickly.

"Flat as a griddle cake and just as dull," Nigel sighed. He sounded like a whiny little boy, in my opinion.

"'Kansas, for the swarming manhood of the British nobility,'" Edwin said bitterly.

"Ha, the swarming manhood problem," Nigel said. "Get rid of primogeniture, and we wouldn't be such a problem."

Swarming manhood? Primogeniture? Mrs. Shaw had said that word before, but I couldn't remember what it was about. It had something to do with Nigel's house—that castle thing—back in England. Or maybe it was his brothers. Nigel was a fifth son. Edwin was a third son. Why were they always talking about this? And why was it a problem?

I was confused, and my feet hurt from balancing on the edge of the trough. I was about to jump down when Edwin said, "On a related subject, old chap, I heard you were all but engaged to Miss Lavinia Peacock."

I froze, my fingers gripping the window ledge.

Tell him, I urged Nigel. *Tell him you've fallen in love with someone else.*

Nigel leaned back and stretched his long legs. "Well . . ."

Well what?

He sighed. "As a matter of fact . . ."

"Hey!" said a voice right next to me.

"Eeep!" I clapped a hand over my mouth to smother a squeal, lost my grip with the other hand, windmilled my arms in the air . . . and fell off the trough, landing in an undignified heap in the dirt.

Eli stood over me, shaking with laughter. "What were

you doing up there?" He put out a hand to help me up.

"Nothing!" I refused his hand and scrambled up. "Mind your own business!"

I stalked off, simmering with indignation at the entire male race. Eli Lewis was an irritating boy who had interrupted at just the wrong moment, and Nigel Ashford . . . Well, let's just say I wasn't sure I liked him.

But Emmeline liked him. That counted for something. And he was rich. That counted twice. At least.

Arithmetic, Cabby. Remember the arithmetic.

Chapter 23

Something was up with Nigel. The next week, he kept pacing around the manor, twisting his long fingers and chewing on the ends of his moustache. One day, I passed the closed door of his study and heard voices inside, his and Lady Ashford's. Nigel's voice was louder, tense and almost shrill. I pressed my ear to the keyhole but couldn't hear what he was saying.

That same evening, I was carrying dinner dishes to the kitchen when I heard a chair scrape hard on the dining room floor, like someone had pushed it back suddenly. "You put Father up to this, didn't you, Mother?" Nigel shouted.

Put his father up to *what*? But Lady Ashford didn't answer, at least that I could hear.

Over the next few days, Nigel spent hours in his study and came out scowling, his fingers ink-stained. His moustache got ragged, he chewed on it so much.

Was it true love? The problem was, I didn't know what true love looked like. Maybe love *always* made people distracted and upset—another reason for avoiding it as long as possible. If only I could consult Emmeline.

One day, I happened to pass Nigel as he came out of his study, biting on his black-stained knuckle. He paused in the hallway like he'd forgotten what he was about to do. Then he stomped out the front door, slamming it behind him.

I peeked into the study. On the polished desk beneath the buffalo head sat a gold-tipped fountain pen and what looked like a letter, held down by a paperweight. I crept into the room—it was for a good cause, remember—tucked my feather duster under my arm, and leaned down for a closer look. Yes, it was a letter, written in an elegant, slanting hand.

My eyes raced over the lines. At first, my brain could make nothing of the shocking words. I tried again, focusing on phrases I could understand: *The hours I have spent with you . . . my ardent zeal and devotion . . . the happiest man in the world.* I checked the signature, and there it was: Nigel Cedrick Saint-James Ashford. My knees turned to jelly.

Even I knew. There was only one reason someone would call himself the happiest man in the world: true love. Nigel was proposing marriage. To . . . Emmeline? The paperweight, a bronze fox on a marble stand, sat right on top of the salutation of the letter. "Dearest—" was all I could see.

Of course it was Emmeline. Only one week earlier, Nigel had kissed my sister in Mr. Meacham's shop. He hadn't spent "hours" with her—more like minutes—but that might be a suitor's exaggeration.

But why would he write to her when he could propose in person? And why hadn't he told anyone: his mother, his friend Edwin, *me?* And why did he look so miserable?

I had to know for sure. My hand crept toward the bronze fox, then stopped. If there was one thing I'd learned while helping my sister in the post office, it was that tampering with the mail was not only a sin but a crime. Although now that I thought about it, the law applied to *opening* someone else's mail, not reading a letter carelessly left out for anyone to see.

I glanced at the buffalo head on the wall, at the leather chair studded with nail heads, out at the empty hallway. My heart beating hard, I picked up the heavy paperweight.

Just then, I heard the front door open. Quick footsteps crossed the foyer and headed my way. Oh, no! I almost wet my drawers.

Somehow, I managed to set down the paperweight, lurch over to the buffalo head, and raise my feather duster. That very second, Nigel stomped into the room.

I looked over my shoulder and choked out, "Spider webs. Bad."

Nigel barely glanced at me. He moved the paperweight, picked up the letter, and hustled back out.

The buffalo's glass eyes seemed to glare into mine. "Snooping will get you nowhere, Catherine Potts," I swore I heard him saying.

"Shut up, you," I answered.

As the days slipped by, I kept at my round of chores like a horse on a threshing machine treadmill, but I was addled and distracted, feverish with heat and suspense. *Was* the letter for Emmeline? Had Nigel sent it yet?

Meanwhile the July sun blazed in a cloudless sky, turning the prairie grass brown and crisp. Inside, Ashford Manor was like an oven. The hot, dry wind blew dust through the open windows. Yours truly got to wipe it up, of course.

One morning, Mrs. Shaw decided to take up the rugs in the foyer and scour the stone floor—have *me* scour the floor, that is. This was unlucky for my poor knees, but lucky for spying, since Nigel happened to be in the drawing room, which was right off the foyer. He was discussing something with Sir Roger Banister and, surprisingly, Mr. H. H. Mortimer of Slocum City.

I sprinkled a mixture of sand and soap onto the floor, sloshed water over it, and set to work with my scrub brush. On all fours, with my skirts hiked up and rags around my knees, I scrubbed my way closer and closer to the open door of the drawing room. I didn't dare look up, but I listened carefully.

"Mr. Ashford, your taste in furnishings is exceptional," I heard Mr. H. H. Mortimer say. The land agent was oily, like Ma said, buttering up the rich guy.

"Exceptional indeed," said Sir Roger in his sarcastic way. "Now, what were we discussing? Oh yes, that our young friend here"—he meant Nigel, I guessed—"is finally awake to the necessity of filthy lucre. Money, as it is more plainly called."

"It's a nuisance, if you ask me," Nigel said. He sounded distressed.

"What?" said Sir Roger a little sharply. "Did you expect the fountain of paternal generosity to keep flowing forever?"

"But to cut off my remittances so abruptly," Nigel groaned.

"Your father . . ." Sir Roger began. But Mr. Shaw came

through the foyer just then, and I had to back away.

After Mr. Shaw passed, I sloshed more water onto the flagstones and tried to make sense of what I'd heard. Nigel's father had cut off his what-do-you-call-ems, his remittances. Remittances meant money, clearly. Lord Ashford had stopped sending Nigel money, and Nigel was upset.

But why had Lord Ashford cut his son off?

I let my mouth fall open, stunned by an incredible idea: *what if Nigel had confessed his love for Emmeline?*

Chapter 24

I picked up my scrub brush and grinned at it. It must be true: Nigel had told his mother that he loved a sod-buster's daughter, a penniless *American*. Lady Ashford had told Lord Ashford, and Lord Ashford had disapproved and stopped sending money. *See,* I lectured the brush, *Nigel does love my sister.* It was perplexing that he hadn't sent Emmeline his marriage proposal—surely I would have heard—but maybe he was carrying it around, too shy to mail it.

I heard Sir Roger talking, so I crept toward the drawing room again, keeping up a light *scritch, scritch* with the brush in case anyone was paying attention.

"As I have mentioned before, my boy," Sir Roger said, "the real money around here isn't in *farming* the land; it's in *owning* the land."

"A truer word was never spoken," put in Mr. H. H. Mortimer.

"The grasshoppers are gone," Sir Roger continued, "and people will be flocking to Kansas before you know it, especially to railroad towns. All wanting farmland, all needing to buy it from the Honorable Nigel Ashford."

"Intriguing idea," said Nigel.

My knees ached, even with rags tied around them,

but I didn't dare move. So, Nigel was interested in the land business. Good for him. Without his remittances, more money might come in handy.

"The trouble is," Nigel went on, "a lot of the land in Kansas is owned by Uncle Sam, as our friends here call their government. Uncle Sam wants to give land away to American homesteaders, not to foreigners like us."

"Try to think creatively, son," Sir Roger said.

"But there are rules, are there not?" Nigel persisted. "About who can get the land assigned for homesteading?"

"That's where a friendly land agent comes in," Sir Roger said with a low chuckle.

Mr. H. H. Mortimer coughed politely. "Yes, I'm happy to be of assistance . . ."

There was a pause, and I sat back on my heels, giving my sore knees a rest. Something about those words, "creatively" and "friendly," didn't sound quite right. But I had no idea what Sir Roger meant.

I heard the sound of crinkling paper. Was Nigel showing them his proposal letter? I had to *see,* not just *hear.* I glanced around the foyer and down the hallway, then stuck my head into the drawing room.

Mr. H. H. Mortimer unfolded something and spread it on a small table. It was too big to be the proposal. Slowly, silently, I crawled further into the room, watching the three men lean over what looked like a map.

Ow! Something whacked me in the ribs. I backed out quickly and looked up. Lady Ashford stood over me, walking stick raised.

"How dare you?" she wheezed, lowering her stick and leaning on it heavily. She glared down at me like I was a cockroach. "How dare you poke your nose into your superiors' business?"

Hot blood rushed to my face. How dare *she*? I was nobody's *inferior*. I scrambled to my feet, glaring at her.

Lady Ashford's gray eyes widened, and our gazes locked. She was taller than me by a foot when she stood up straight. Bent over her walking stick, she met me eye to eye.

I clenched my fists. I took a breath. I said . . . nothing.

You didn't scream at sick old ladies, no matter how angry they made you. I dropped my eyes with a sigh.

"I shall tell Mrs. Shaw to cancel your next day off," Lady Ashford said coolly. "And pull your skirts down." She started to cough. "I . . . I won't have you . . . disgracing my household." With that, she tottered off, her stick tapping with every step.

All that day, I tried to shrug it off, the poke in the ribs, the humiliation, the punishment. A mark on my rib I could take; I'd had plenty of bruises before. Losing my Sunday morning off was bad, but now that I thought about it, I supposed I deserved it.

It was that word "superiors" that really hurt. It throbbed in my mind like a bruise. Lady Ashford hadn't said it like an insult, just a fact: she was superior, and I was inferior.

Old doubts flooded my mind. Maybe it *was* crazy, imagining that the Ladyship's son would marry his housemaid's sister. Of course he would, I tried to tell myself. Of course he *will*. But I couldn't shake the gloomy feeling.

The gloom only darkened the next morning when I pulled on the black dress. My brooch wasn't fastened to the collar! I checked my other dresses, tore back the covers of my bed, flung everything out of my drawers, but the brooch wasn't there. I raced down the stairs, flew through the kitchen, the scullery, the hallways—no brooch.

Pa had given me the brooch for Christmas last year. He pinned it to my collar and stood back to look at me. "My little Cabbage looks like a duchess," he said. I wasn't one for fancy things, but I felt so proud that day.

Stupid, stupid Cabby. Why hadn't I been more careful? Now, part of *me* was lost.

I moped through my work, until Mrs. Shaw asked if I was sick. I *was* sick: sick of Ashford Manor, sick of the Ashfords. I ached to be myself again: Cabby, not Catherine. I wanted to feel the July wind in my hair, scrape my hoe into the dirt, milk Lissie, and scratch our horses between the ears. I wanted to tease my little brothers and whisper secrets with my sister, my best friend. I wanted to be *home.*

Why did the grasshoppers have to come? Why did we have to worry about money? And what if Pa really did give up our claim? Where would we go this time? America was a big country—I pictured the Potts family blowing across it like tumbleweeds, snagging here and there but never settling anywhere. Even worse, I pictured another family moving onto *our* claim, our 160 acres of prairie with its brave little patch of corn. Our own land, abandoned to strangers. My first real home, gone. These months of housemaiding, for nothing.

Chapter 25

Wheat harvest started the next day, and I was too busy to mope or to puzzle over what Nigel was thinking. It was a relief, actually.

Mr. Rouse hired a team of men for the reaping, which meant they had to be fed, which meant even more work than usual. At breakfast, they all crowded into the kitchen, wolfing down gigantic amounts of bacon and eggs and coffee. At lunch, they were back, eyes bloodshot from the dust, and hungry again. Some of them made faces at Mrs. Shaw's steak-and-kidney pudding, but they ate all of it, washing it down with even more coffee. There were piles of dishes to wash.

In the afternoon, Mrs. Shaw sent me out to the fields with Mr. Shaw, who carried two heavy water buckets while I carried pails of hot scones wrapped in towels. I didn't mind the walk at all. As we got closer to the fields, I could see yellow dust floating in the air and smell the scent of ripe wheat. It actually smelled like bread, and I thought it was the best scent in the world.

In the field, Nigel's plow horses, William and Robert, pulled the reaping machine with powerful steps, their big heads bobbing up and down. The long blades of the machine turned with a steady *clack-clack,* mowing down the golden wheat and pushing it onto a chute. Cut wheat slid off the chute onto the ground, and men hurried behind the machine, binding the stalks into sheaves.

"It's beautiful, isn't it?" I said impulsively to Mr. Shaw. I meant it. I loved the ripe wheat and the clacking machine and the wiggly line of wheat sheaves stretching through the stubble. I could hardly wait to tell Pa we should plant the north field in wheat instead of corn.

"You're a strange sort o' girl, missy," Mr. Shaw said, looking at me worriedly. "I thought you young ones only liked ribbons and frippery."

"Not all of us," I answered. That was something I loved about Kansas, or at least my part of Kansas: if you didn't care about frippery, it didn't matter much. Here, a girl could get dirt under her fingernails—in fact, she pretty much had to.

I, Cabby Potts, was a Kansas girl. And I meant to keep it that way.

"Be a good girl and cut up this rhubarb for me, Cabby," Mrs. Shaw said late that night. "I've got to check the cellar for potatoes."

I was mighty tired, and I'd never had much use for rhubarb, but I couldn't say no. I washed the long red stalks and sat at the kitchen table. Chop, chop went my knife. Chop . . . chop . . . until my head nodded and I fell asleep right over the rhubarb.

"Cabby?" said a voice.

"Sorry, Mrs. Shaw," I mumbled. "I'm awake now."

But it was Nigel who stared down at me. "Good evening. How is your, er, family?"

"Fine, I guess," I said, still half asleep.

Then it hit me: he was asking about Emmeline. At last. Maybe he'd been waiting for a private moment to ask me the best way to propose.

"My *sister* is . . . she's fine," I added lamely.

Nigel fiddled with the end of his moustache. It was understandable he'd be nervous, I supposed, talking about a delicate matter like love. "Good, good, glad to hear it," he said. "And your family's homestead, how is that going?"

I blinked, confused.

"What I mean to say is, you mentioned the matter of some, er, difficulties?" Nigel's eyes focused somewhere around my chin.

So it seems Nigel had heard it too, when I'd blabbed the story of my family's difficulties at breakfast the other morning. Well, it was only fair he knew the details. He shouldn't think Emmeline had anything to hide. So I explained again about the grasshoppers, and losing all our crops, and how we had another year before we could prove up on our claim. Nigel was surprisingly interested, asking about things like commutation and affidavits of something-or-other. I didn't know half of what he was talking about, and all the time I kept thinking how to steer the conversation back to my sister.

"Are many of the locals in the same pecuniary position?" Nigel asked.

"Huh? I mean—excuse me?"

"Are they in financial difficulty as well?"

I couldn't think why he'd want to know this, but I told him about the Prouty boarding house being empty, and the homesteaders who'd gone back East, and the sign that said "Eaten by Grasshoppers." My mind kept skipping back to Emmeline. Maybe Nigel was timid, afraid to move too fast. How could I light his fire, marriage-wise? Well . . . he was a competitive person, right? He liked card games and horse races and croquet and cricket. Maybe if he thought he had competition for her hand, he'd move a little quicker.

I cleared my throat. In spite of the spying I'd done lately, lying didn't come easy. "By the way," I said, trying to sound casual, "my sister has a suitor. I think he's *very* interested." This was a flat-out fib.

Now Nigel looked right at me. "Really?"

I didn't intend to be specific about who this mythical suitor was. To my amazement, Nigel snapped his fingers. "It's the shopkeeper, isn't it?"

"What?" I was dumbfounded.

"That big oaf of a shopkeeper," he repeated hotly. "Anyone could tell he's in love with her."

I struggled to keep my mouth from falling open. Fortunately, at that moment Mrs. Shaw bustled into the kitchen holding potatoes in her apron. Nigel hesitated a moment, then went out.

"What did *'e* want in 'ere?" Mrs. Shaw asked.

"He, well, he wanted . . . I don't know," I stammered. I was all out of lies.

Mrs. Shaw shook her head, and I went back to chopping rhubarb, my mind reeling. Was it true about Knee-High? Now that I thought about it, he was kind to everybody, but he was extra nice to Emmeline, showing up whenever he thought she needed him. Like when I was crying in the post office and when Lady Ashford was sick. He turned red every time he looked at her, and he got upset when he saw Nigel kissing her. How could I have missed it? Even Moonbeam, Knee-High's cat, saw it. That's why Moonbeam didn't like Emmeline. Of course, Nigel was right: Knee-High Meacham was in love with my sister.

For a minute I felt terrible. I really liked Knee-High. He was my friend and maybe the nicest man I knew, besides Pa. I didn't like to think of him disappointed in love, as the stories put it. But what if he proposed to Emmeline and she said yes?

This is no time to get sentimental, Cabby Potts, I lectured myself, chop-chopping firmly with my knife. *Remember the arithmetic.*

As soon as Mrs. Shaw dismissed me, I found a pen full of ink, hurried up to my room, pulled my carpetbag from under the bed, and extracted the writing paper Knee-High had given me.

"Sorry, Mr. Meacham," I whispered. Then, writing so fast the ink splattered all over the paper, I wrote:

Dear Emmeline,
I hope you are well. And Ma and Pa and the boys. I am writing to say that Mr. Nigel Ashford asks about you ALL THE TIME. He wishes to be made the happiest man in the world.
Your faithful sister,
Cabby
To be sure she got the message, I added:

P.S. If you happen to get any other proposals of marriage, please say no.

The next morning, I put my letter on the tray by the front door and watched as Mr. Shaw carried it off.

There. The deed was done.

Chapter 26

The deed was done, and I felt . . . just a tad uneasy. As the day went along—another busy one because of the wheat harvest—I kept remembering how my letter turned my *guesses* into *facts*. I imagined Emmeline tearing the envelope open, pictured the happiness on her face. Probably she'd even tell Ma and Pa, since I had practically guaranteed her a proposal from Nigel. For some reason, that idea made me queasy.

The wheat harvest lasted two more days, and I shoved the uneasiness out of my mind. On the last day, I washed a mile-high stack of sticky breakfast plates, then Mrs. Shaw told me the men wouldn't be back for lunch. "Milady won't be back either," she said, giving me a significant look. "She's spending the day with Lady Banister. Master's gone, too."

"Oh?" I said.

"So if a certain 'ousemaid were to relax a bit, well, who would be the wiser? You can have the rest of the day off."

"Really?" I threw my towel into the air.

"You've been working 'ard, lass, and I don't see the point of canceling your time off. Just don't be spying at any more doors."

"I won't," I said, feeling the sting of embarrassment. "Can . . . can I go to the stable?"

"I guess so, but don't be stealing any of your Master's 'orses, neither."

"I won't," I said again. "Thank you, Ma'am!"

I ran upstairs, changed into my own dress, and hurried to the corral. Three-Legs trotted over to see me, and I stroked his neck . . . keeping my eyes open for a certain Eli, also known as *Kehimi,* Prairie Dog. When he came out of the stable, widening his eyes at the sight of me, I felt a ridiculous urge to smooth my hair. I didn't, though—I wasn't that kind of girl.

"Hey, Cabby," Eli said, "I was just going to look for you."

It was my turn to be surprised. "What for?"

"Guess where Mr. Ashford is."

"Mr. Ashford? Where?"

"Gone to *your* claim. Yesterday, he sent me out there with a note, and now he's going there himself."

"Wh-why didn't you tell me?" I sputtered.

"I *am* telling you. I thought you'd be happy. Didn't you think Mr. Ashford was interested in your sister? Maybe you're right."

I could barely hear him, smacked by waves of emotions. First came triumph: Nigel was going to propose to Emmeline! Then came disbelief: could it really be true?

One thing I knew, I had to be there. Maybe it wasn't logical, but I felt absolutely certain. For my brilliant inspiration to succeed, I, Cabby Potts, had to witness the proposal.

"When did he leave?" I demanded, grabbing Eli's shirt front. "Did he say anything? What did the note say?"

"Whoa, slow down, Cabby. He left maybe an hour ago, he didn't say why he was going, and I don't know what the note said."

"Eli, can you drive me home? Please? I have the day off."

He backed away. "Have you gone crazy? I'd get fired. Besides, Mr. Ashford took the buggy."

I looked at Three-Legs, who snorted in a friendly way.

"Oh no you don't, Cabby Potts."

Of course I couldn't take Three-Legs. I promised Mrs. Shaw not to steal any more horses. I sagged against the corral fence, out of ideas.

"You know," Eli said slowly, "if you really want to go home, there is a way."

I didn't bother to straighten up. "What? Fly?"

"No. Take the train."

"I don't have money for a train ticket."

"Listen," Eli said. "Are you serious about this?" He glanced up at the sun. "Almost time. Come on, we're taking a walk to Prince Albert."

A half hour later, Eli and I stood in the doorway of a coal shed not far from the Prince Albert train depot. "What am I supposed to do again?" I said.

"Like I've been saying," he replied, "the train will slow down right about here, and the conductor will toss the mail sacks off. Then you look for a boxcar with an open door and hop on really quick, before anyone sees you."

"Just like that?"

"Sure. I've done it plenty of times. Haven't you ever been on a train?"

"Of course, in a *passenger* car." I didn't mention that it was six years ago. Since then, the Potts family had been too inconvenienced for train tickets. I also didn't mention that trains made me anxious, to put it mildly. They were big, and loud, and fast. "I . . . I'm not sure this is a good idea. What if . . .?"

Just then a train whistle shrieked. The locomotive barreled toward the depot, belching steam and roaring like a charging buffalo. I backed deeper into the shed. "I can't do it."

"Sure you can," Eli said. "You threw a rattlesnake over a wall, remember?" As the train slowed with a squeal of brakes, he crouched, watching the cars roll by. He grabbed my hand. "That one! Come on!"

We dashed together to an open boxcar as it rolled slowly by. Eli jumped, I jumped. Just like that, I was aboard a moving train. Good gracious, I had my arms wrapped right around Eli Lewis's neck. How did that happen?

"You okay?" he said. I nodded and pulled away slowly, feeling my cheeks burn.

"Don't forget, you've got to jump off when the train slows down, before you get into Slocum City. Got it?"

I nodded again, and Eli hurried to the edge of the moving car, turning around to flash me a grin. "Good luck!" Just as the train began to pick up speed, he leaped out the open door.

I sat down shakily, realizing with a pang that I hadn't thanked him. I would do it tonight, when I got back to Ashford Manor. "Thank you, *Kehimi*, my friend," I would say—as long as no one could hear me say his Kiowa name.

The boxcar jostled and bumped. I sat with my hands flat on the dirty floor while the countryside rushed by. Watching the telegraph poles flicking past—one, two, three—made me a little sick, so I had to stop watching. Thinking about what lay ahead made me even more terrified: would Nigel actually propose? Was this really happening? In the end I put my head in my hands, shut my eyes, and tried not to throw up as the train hurtled toward Slocum City.

It seemed like only minutes later when I heard the brakes screech. I stood up in a panic and teetered to the open doorway. The prairie was still rolling by so fast. The whistle blew, the brakes screeched again, and I felt the *whump whump* of the wheels slowing down.

I had to jump.

I couldn't jump.

Now, Cabby!

I jumped. *Crash!* I rolled down the low slope, tumbling like a one-person avalanche. I caught my shoe in the hem of my dress and heard it rip—drat!

When I stopped rolling, I sat up cautiously, spitting dirt out of my mouth. No bones broken, and nobody had seen me. So far, so good, except for the ripped dress and the fact that I still had to hoof it three miles to my house.

I was drenched with sweat, not to mention anxiety, by the time I stood outside the door of my own sod house. Before I could decide whether to knock, the door opened and I was face to face with Pa. He wore a clean, ironed shirt, his eyes twinkling like he knew a secret he couldn't wait to tell. *Oh boy, here we go.*

"Why, Cabbage, we weren't expecting to see you," Pa said, hugging me. "Mr. Ashford brought you?" He peered around me, looking for a horse and buggy.

"Um, no . . ."

"How did you get here?" Ma squeezed around Pa to squint at me suspiciously. "What's going on, Cabby?"

She had reason to be suspicious, I guess, but it still grated like sandpaper. It was thanks to me—and true love—that the Potts family was about to be rescued from serious inconvenience.

I took a breath and looked her right in the eye. "Oh, hi, Ma. I got a ride from Mr. Mortimer. He was at Ashford Manor, and he gave me a ride as far as town. I have the day off." Some parts of the story were true. Small parts.

"Well, I don't like you begging rides from people," Ma sniffed. "What happened to your dress? And your face?"

"I, uh . . ." I hadn't thought about that part.

"Never mind that now. Go wash your face, quickly."

I splashed some well water on my face then hurried inside, wishing for the hundredth time that I had my brooch. It would make me look more respectable. The table was covered with Ma's best linen tablecloth and spread with our best—though chipped—crockery plates. Emmeline stood by the window, wearing her rose-colored Sunday calico, with her chestnut hair swept up and pinned with Ma's pearl combs. She looked so shy and pretty and grown-up it made me want to cry. She caught me by both hands. "Cabby, I'm happy you're here! Do . . . do I look all right?"

I was stammering out an answer when she turned back to the window. "It's Nigel. He's here!"

Chapter 27

If Nigel was surprised to see me when Pa welcomed him inside, he didn't show it. Or maybe he didn't give much thought to how housemaids got around. A few minutes later, we were all seated at the table, Pa beaming proudly at the head.

"Won't you have a biscuit, Mr. Ashford?" Ma said, her voice formal.

"Mrs. Potts, you shouldn't have fussed," Nigel said. He wore a black checked waistcoat and a gray tie. He looked handsome, as always, but not as fancy as you might have expected. He smiled, but his smile didn't seem to reach his eyes. He hadn't looked at Emmeline once.

Everyone watched as Nigel took a biscuit, broke it open, and scooped a big glob of butter onto his knife.

"You're taking too much butter!" Jesse blurted out. In our family, this was almost a crime.

"Jesse!" Emmeline scolded.

Jesse hung his head. Nigel looked around the table in confusion and gulped down the biscuit without any butter at all. In the silence that followed, the expectancy was so thick you could almost see it. I could hear Snuff scratching himself outside the door.

Finally Nigel wiped his hands on a napkin. "Mr. Potts

. . ." he began. A bead of sweat stood out on his forehead.

I held my breath, not daring to look at Emmeline. Now Nigel would ask Pa for a private talk, when he would ask for Emmeline's hand, or at least for permission to court her. That's how these things were done, right?

"Er, Mr. Potts. I wonder if I might propose something to you."

That was a funny way to put it. "Shall we step outside?" Pa said hesitantly.

"No need," Nigel said.

No need? Emmeline looked at Pa with worried, questioning eyes. He smiled at her and patted her hand.

"The fact of the matter is," Nigel went on, shifting in his wooden chair, "I have become aware of your family's, er, financial difficulties."

What?

Nigel cleared his throat. "I am also aware that you have one more year before you can prove up, as they say, on this claim." He spoke slowly and carefully, like this was something he had practiced.

Silence. Emmeline went as still as a china doll. Even Snuff stopped scratching. Everyone stared at Nigel.

"I would like to propose something that may be of mutual benefit," he went on quickly. He looked only at Pa. "I am seeking land in this area, and this parcel seems like a pleasant one. I will offer you one hundred dollars for this claim, payable immediately. You will go to the land office, formally exercise your commutation right, and then sign the title over to me."

"You want our land?" Pa said, like he wasn't sure of his hearing. "That's why you've come?"

Nigel wanted our land. At first, I couldn't even understand the words, like they were nonsense syllables with no meaning, *la la la.* I felt like I'd been picked up by a tornado, and everything was upside down and backwards. Nigel wasn't here to propose? He wanted us to give up our claim? It didn't make sense.

Pa blinked a few times and shook his head like he was shaking his stuck thoughts loose. "How much did you say?" he finally asked.

I couldn't believe he was actually considering this. "Pa! Don't listen to him!"

"Don't, Pa, please!" Orin cried.

"Hush, children," Ma said. Her mouth was set in a grim line, and she hadn't taken her eyes off Nigel. Beside her, my poor sister sat silently, her eyes dark pools.

"As I mentioned, Mr. Potts," Nigel said carefully, "I am prepared to offer one hundred dollars for . . ."

"Mr. Ashford," Ma said coolly. "Why would you want this particular quarter-section when you have land of your own?"

Good question, Ma.

"Why, Mrs. Potts," Nigel said, "this is a fine piece of land, with some improvements already made." That didn't exactly answer the question. "Besides, considering your family's, er, delicate position," he went on, "perhaps you're asking the wrong question. Consider how this could benefit *you.*"

Pa rubbed his hand through his hair. "It's a generous offer, Martha," he murmured.

"Pa, no!" I said. Pa *must not* listen to Nigel. Right then I didn't care if he was offering one hundred dollars, or one million.

"*Is* it a generous offer?" Ma said sharply, ignoring my outburst. "Mr. Ashford, you do know that the commutation rate is one dollar and twenty five cents an acre, which adds up to *two* hundred dollars?"

"I am aware, Mrs. Potts," Nigel said quickly, like he had expected this question. "But are you likely to find someone to pay you two hundred dollars?"

"Furthermore," Ma said, "homesteading laws don't allow us to transfer title to you, not unless we pay the full two hundred dollars to . . ."

"My *dear* Mrs. Potts," Nigel interrupted, "would I suggest a course of action that wasn't legal?" The sweat glistened on his forehead. "There are always exceptions to the laws, certain conditions, you understand . . ." When Ma said nothing, he pulled a piece of paper and a pen from his pocket. "Just in case any, shall we say, *inquiries* arise, I'll ask you to sign this document saying the relinquishment was of your own free will, et cetera, et cetera. A mere trifle."

Ma and Pa looked at each other. "I don't know . . ." Pa said.

Nigel took a breath and smiled like someone who's about to play the winning card. For the first time, he looked at Emmeline—only not exactly *at* her, I noticed. More like in her direction. "In light of the, er, *close association* between my family and yours, you can rest assured I have your best interest at heart."

I felt like the air was sucked out of my lungs. I knew what Nigel was hinting: that there was something special between him and Emmeline. He wanted us to think he cared for Emmeline so we would accept his offer and not worry. But I knew now it wasn't true. Everything in Nigel's face and manner said it: *liar, liar, liar.*

It's hard to think when your head is pounding, but I tried to see where I had gone astray, where I'd added up my sums and gotten them wrong . . . There was Nigel's father cutting off his remittances, for one thing: I had jumped to a conclusion, assuming it was because he confessed love for Emmeline. But hadn't he said the reason himself? Lady Ashford didn't like his extravagant ways, had complained to Lord Ashford. Lord Ashford had cut off the money, and now he needed a way to make some of his own. I didn't understand why our claim was so important to him, but one thing was clear: *love* didn't enter the picture.

Did Emmeline see it? She leaned toward Nigel, shy hope replacing the despair on her face. No, she didn't see it.

I felt the blood pound behind my eyes, and my hands clenched on the table edge.

"Well, Martha, what do you think?" Pa said slowly. "We do need the money."

I jumped to my feet, my chair toppling into the bureau behind me. "Pa!" I yelled. "Don't listen to Mr. Ashford. He's a liar!"

—Part 5—

A Pair of Scoundrels

Chapter 28

"What's this, Cabby?" Ma barked.

Pa put out a hand. "Cabby, sweetheart," he said soothingly.

"Mr. Ashford doesn't care one bit about 'our interests'!" I shouted. "I heard him talking to Mr. Mortimer and Sir Roger. They talked about buying land and homesteading laws . . . and things."

"Well, what of it?" Nigel said, his voice low and even. His face had gone pale, and his nostrils flared with fury. "How dare you accuse me of lying?"

I looked from Ma to Pa. "See, he lost his remittances, and he needs money and . . . this whole thing doesn't make sense!" I knew I wasn't making sense. I just knew something was wrong with Nigel's offer. Why would he want *our* land? Why would he ask us to sign that paper? It was like an animal had crawled into the walls of the house and died—I couldn't find it, but I could smell it.

There was something else I had to say. "All that stuff about *close association,* that's a lie too." Emmeline looked at me and gasped. I was hurting her, but I had to go on. My mind desperately putting the pieces together, adding up the sums, I said, "I saw a letter Mr. Ashford wrote. It was to . . ."

I hesitated, hating to say it. "It was to Lavinia Peacock. He asked her to marry him."

I looked at Nigel. Even now, he could deny it. He could say, "No, you've got it all wrong. It's Emmeline I want to marry. See, right here in my pocket, it's the proposal I meant to send."

He didn't say that, though. He glared at me across the table. "*You* have been *reading my mail*?"

So it was true.

"You don't even like Lavinia!" I shouted. I knew I had crossed a line, but I didn't care. "She isn't half as nice as my sister!"

I had been wrong about Nigel, dead wrong. He was not the hero of my family's story. He was the cruel, treacherous *villain.* He had kissed my sister only to abandon her and propose to someone else, someone he wasn't in love with.

And now he was going after our quarter-section of Kansas land.

"Cabby!" Pa said. He had his arm around Emmeline, who shook with silent sobs.

Nigel stood up slowly, staring down at me. "*Your employment in my household is terminated,*" he said, spitting out the words one at a time. He turned to Pa. "Mr. Potts, I'll be in the land office tomorrow at nine. I fully expect you to be there as well, when you *will* accept my offer." He grabbed his hat, jammed it on his head, and barged out.

Nigel was barely out the door when the storm broke. "Cabby, why'd you have to get yourself fired?" Orin yelled. Ma and Pa's voices joined in. "Never seen you behave like this . . . reading your employer's mail . . . I thought better of you, daughter." Even Jesse looked mad at me.

Emmeline's voice cut through with a cold fury I had never heard before. "How could you? How could you speak to Nigel like that?"

Stung, I couldn't help defending myself. "I'm sorry . . . but he . . . he's a rat."

She stood up, her face as pale as paper. "Nigel is *not* a rat!"

"But he's trying to take our land!"

"And he *does* love me!" My sister's glare burned into my face.

"Now, Emmeline," Pa said.

"It's true! You're wrong about him, all of you. I'm the only one who understands him, and I know he loves me." She leaned across the table to face me, eyes blazing. "I hate you, Cabby!" she yelled.

I felt my legs buckle, and big sobs rose in my throat. I turned blindly and stumbled out the door. Snuff ran to meet me in the yard, whining at my skirt like he knew something was up. "Come on, boy," I choked, crying so hard I could barely see. I pushed through the grasses until I found the spot: a room-sized depression in the flat prairie, where the grasses mixed with sunflowers and purple poppy-mallows. It was mine and Em's secret spot, a place where the buffalo used to roll.

I trampled down some sunflower stalks and flopped on my belly in the bottom of the hollow, sobbing. I felt lonelier than I ever had at Ashford Manor. Everything had gone so wrong, and somehow it was all my fault. My stupid, childish dream—brilliant inspiration, what a joke.

I thought I would cry forever, but it turned out that

wasn't possible. The sun beat down on me, even here in the buffalo wallow, and the grasses made me itch. I sat up after a while, hoping I'd see my sister looking over the edge. "Come on back, Cabby, I don't really hate you," she'd say.

She wasn't there, of course, so I wiped my hot, swollen face with the hem of my dress, climbed out, and slunk toward the house. I saw Ma and Pa standing by the well, talking. Pa said something and Ma sank down on the wall of the well, her head in her hands. Oh, no.

When I rushed up, Pa kept talking like I wasn't even there. "I *know,* Martha, it's what I always say." He sounded almost happy. "But I'm right this time. And we wouldn't have to go to Kansas City, not if you don't want to. I hear there's money in the timber business out West. Oregon, to be specific."

Ma didn't even lift her head from her hands.

Pa paced around the well, going around me like I was just a stump in his way, and I didn't dare say anything. "With a hundred dollars," he said, "we'd have enough to get set up. Think of it, Martha, a land full of trees, after this barren place."

How could he be excited about giving up our land— and for less than it was really worth?

Ma answered him, but I could barely take in her words. I felt like a slow-moving landslide was rolling toward our little house and there was nothing I could do to stop it. By the time Ma and Pa headed back inside, somehow Ma had agreed to sell our land to Nigel. Or maybe not agreed, exactly. More like got swept along. Either way, it was decided that Pa would meet Nigel at the land office and accept his offer. If my parents had wanted to punish me, this was the worst thing they could have thought of.

Chapter 29

All night long, Emmeline kept her back to me. I woke up before the sun had properly risen, and she still faced away from me, sleeping or pretending to sleep. I slipped out to the necessary in my thin shift, my nightgown being at Ashford Manor. I had ached to be home every night when I was there, but now everything was ruined.

When I stepped out of the smelly privy, I saw Ma opening the door of the chicken coop. Her chickens bustled out, and she tossed them some feed. In the soft morning light, and with her hair down, she looked a lot like Emmeline.

Suddenly I wanted to make her understand. "Hey, Ma," I called.

She straightened up. "What is it, Cabby?"

"I'm sorry." My throat hurt, and my voice felt thick. "I'm sorry I got fired, and . . . everything."

"*Everything* is not your fault," Ma said. She shook a few crumbs out of her apron. "But I'm disappointed in you, child. I thought you understood how important your job was." She ducked into the coop. Conversation over.

"But I was trying to *help*!" I said.

Ma emerged with two brown eggs in her hand. "How,

exactly, were you trying to help?"

"I tried to get Nigel to fall in love with Em. I thought . . . I thought he would, you know, support us, buy us stuff."

"If that's not the most foolish notion I've ever heard . . ."

I tried to explain. I told her about my inspiration . . . and Lavinia wanting to see a genuine sod hut . . . and Lady Ashford getting sick . . . and the kiss . . . and the proposal I thought was for Emmeline. It did sound like a foolish notion now, like I didn't know a fairy story from a true one. But it felt right to tell her the truth.

Ma listened all the way through. When I was done, she put out a hand to touch my shoulder. It was a tiny thing, but it was something. Then she sighed. "What difference does all this make now? Go on inside, we need to leave soon."

An hour later, the chores were done, and my parents and sister and I climbed into the wagon. I begged to stay home with the boys, but Ma and Pa said the boys were old enough to stay on their own, and I needed to help Emmeline in the post office. By that they meant keep an eye on her, I guessed. She sure was acting strangely, moping around and staring into space like she was gazing into a certain some-one's eyes.

Lightning and Bolt plodded toward Slocum City as slowly they always did, but not slowly enough for me. As I watched the sluggish swish of their tails, my mind swung to folks in town and the curious questions they would ask. From them my thoughts turned to Eli—I hadn't even thanked him for helping me get on the train—and then to

Mr. and Mrs. Shaw and Lady Ashford. What had Nigel told them? What did they think of me? My stomach twisted and curdled like I had drunk sour milk.

Well, Ma was right—what people thought didn't matter now anyway. My sister's hopes were blasted, and she hated me. By the end of the day, our land would belong to the *Dis*honorable Nigel Ashford.

Pa dropped Emmeline and me outside Nehemiah Meacham's General Store and Post Office. Immediately, Mrs. Snopes, busybody-in-chief of Slocum City, scuttled up. She wore her black hat topped with the rusty-looking stuffed bird, and her little eyes glinted suspiciously from underneath. "Well, Cabby Potts," she demanded, "what are *you* doing here?"

"Just home for a while," I mumbled. I wished Emmeline would say something to help me out, but she didn't, of course.

"Hmm," Mrs. Snopes said. "Well, I'd like to have a word with that English Lordy of yours. He still hasn't paid for our broken window. Doesn't that take nerve . . ."

She stopped suddenly, staring across the street as Nigel Ashford came out of the Grand Paris Hotel, settled his hat on his head, and moseyed up the sidewalk toward the land office.

"Aha!" Mrs. Snopes cackled. She scurried after Nigel. Emmeline hesitated for a second then scurried after *her.*

I ran to catch my sister. "What are you doing? Ma said to go straight to the post office."

She pulled her arm out of my grip. "I just have to talk to Nigel for one minute. Don't tell Ma and Pa, please?"

I didn't know what to do. If I fetched Ma and Pa, she'd

never speak to me again, ever. But it couldn't be a good idea, her chasing after Nigel.

In the end, I trailed behind, hoping maybe Ma and Pa would show up quickly enough to put a stop to this. But no such luck. Fleet as an antelope, Emmeline ran past Mrs. Snopes and caught up to Nigel just outside the land office. I couldn't hear what she said, but I saw her clutch her hands together, saw Nigel draw away from her. Oh, no.

I came closer, drawn to the spectacle like I was magnetized. "What's this? What's it all about?" Mrs. Snopes cackled in my ear. I ignored her.

"Nigel, is it true?" Emmeline cried. "Are you going to marry Lavinia?"

"Miss Potts," Nigel replied, "I'm afraid my matrimonial intentions are no concern of yours." His words were calm, but he pulled at the collar of his shirt like it was too tight for him.

"How can you say that? I thought, I understood . . ."

Nigel pulled himself straighter. "Anything you might have *thought* was entirely of your own invention. There is no understanding between you and me."

"Oh, Nigel!" Emmeline wailed. "Don't you love me at all?" She swayed on her feet, and I was afraid she'd collapse.

"Pull yourself together, Miss Potts," Nigel said, his voice shaking a little. I noticed he couldn't look at my sister. "I'll thank you to stop badgering me."

Emmeline started to sob, covering her face with her hands.

I stood paralyzed. I was no good in romantic disasters. Fortunately, Ma and Pa arrived just then, rushing up to Emmeline on both sides. Nigel turned very red, but he tipped his hat at my sister like they'd been having a pleasant chat. "Now if you'll excuse me, I have some business with your father." He disappeared into the land office.

Emmeline buried her face in Pa's shoulder, sobbing. Pa's face went as dark as a thundercloud. Gently, he pulled away from her and followed Nigel into the office.

"Cabby," Ma said, taking my sister by the hand, "go ask Mr. Meacham to take care of the post office. Tell him Emmeline is unwell." Meanwhile Mrs. Snopes cackled and grumbled, but no one paid her any mind.

A few minutes later, Ma, Emmeline, and I were back in the wagon, heading for home. Pa would have to walk. Emmeline sat on the seat with Ma, slumped like a potato sack. I sat in the wagon bed, trying to think of anything other than the scene I had just witnessed. But what else was there to think about?

Lightning and Bolt poked along even slower than usual. So we hadn't gone far when someone hailed us from behind the wagon. "Can a fellow have a ride?" It was Pa. He trotted up as Ma reined in the horses. My heart sank even further—so the thing was done.

"That was fast," Ma said, staring straight ahead.

"Yes, yes it was," Pa panted.

"Is everything finished?"

Pa coughed and scratched his neck like the sun was making him itch. "Yes. No. Sort of."

Ma swung around to look at him. "What are you saying?"

"Actually, to tell you the truth . . . I didn't do it."

"What?" Ma and I cried together. Emmeline said nothing.

Pa looked up at Ma sheepishly. "How could I give up our claim to that . . . that *man!* I'm a father, after all. No one is cruel to my daughter then tries to take my land."

I stared at Pa, not quite able to take this in.

"Oh, Albert," Ma said. I couldn't tell if she was happy or mad. "What did you say to him?"

"Well, I suggested, politely of course, that Mr. Ashford use his one hundred dollars to buy a boat ticket back to England."

"That's the way, Pa!" I couldn't help crowing.

"Hush, Cabby. What did *he* say to *that?*" Ma said.

"Let's just say it wasn't suitable for your tender ears."

"Oh, Albert!" Ma said again. Now I could tell she was happy. She leaned over the edge of the wagon and kissed Pa on the forehead. "You sentimental idiot!"

Pa looked up at her with a grin.

"So we can stay, Pa?" I demanded. "Keep our claim?"

Pa's grin faded. "We'll see, Cabby."

Chapter 30

The next morning, I jumped out of bed early, determined to be the most useful daughter the world had ever seen. That wouldn't solve our problems, but I reckoned it couldn't hurt. I would milk the cow, water the horses, and tend the garden. I'd tote buckets, wash dishes, and clean the chicken coop. If I was feeling heroic, I would even do the mending. Hopefully, all that napkin hemming at Ashford Manor had improved my needlework.

I had just finished milking Lissie when Pa came out and asked me to help him plow a firebreak. He'd seen some distant prairie fires, he said, and they were bound to come closer.

"Sure, Pa!" I said. I almost skipped to the shed. I figured he couldn't hate me too much if he was asking me for help.

We hitched the horses and dragged the plow to the edge of the claim. I walked at Lightning's head, keeping the team going straight while Pa steered the plow through the dry sod, the roots going *pop, pop* as the steel blade ripped through them. The idea was to turn over a strip wide enough to stop a wind-blown fire. It was hard, heavy work, and Lightning and Bolt were covered with sweat and foam before we made two turns.

"I haven't seen a cloud in weeks," Pa said, tugging at his sweat-soaked shirt as we stopped to rest the horses. He laughed. "Welcome to Kansas. If the grasshoppers don't eat your crops, the fire will burn them up."

"But you like it here, don't you?" I glanced nervously at him from under my sunbonnet brim. "I mean, except for grasshoppers and fires."

"Sure I do, Cabbage," Pa said. "Sure, I like it here." But he didn't sound convinced. "Come on, let's finish this before the sun gets high."

When I got inside—after pouring an entire bucket of water over my head—Emmeline was crying *again.* "Ma, I *have* to quit my job," she sobbed. "How can I show my face in town? Everyone will cast aspersions on me!"

She kind of had a point, considering the spectacle she had made of herself yesterday, but I knew better than to say so.

Ma wheeled on Emmeline, her eyes practically throwing sparks. "Grow up, child! Do you think you have the luxury of quitting the post office because of some wounded *feelings*? For fifty cents a week in supplies, you'd better let people cast all the aspersions they want."

"Yes, Ma," Emmeline said in a small voice. She turned back to the stove, stirring the beans mechanically. Ma grabbed a bucket and marched out the door.

I followed Ma outside to the well, watching her crank the handle with her back to me. Her dress was ragged at the hem and patched at the elbows with unmatched pieces of calico.

Ma had always worn decent dresses before the grasshoppers. We were inconvenienced even then, but we had store-bought coffee occasionally, and Pa was at least thinking about buying lumber for a real wooden house. I stood watching Ma, the satisfaction I had felt while I was plowing with Pa evaporating like the dew.

For the first time, I was the tiniest bit sorry I had yelled at Nigel Ashford. For two dollars a week, maybe I should have kept my mouth shut and respected my employer.

On the other hand, would respecting Nigel have stopped him from going after our land? I would never be sorry I had stood up to him about that.

I walked to the well and took the handle from Ma. The bucket was a long way down, which meant the water level was low. "Ma," I said as I turned the handle, "what are we going to do now? Without my pay, I mean?"

She straightened up and rubbed her back. "You really want to know, Cabby?"

"Yes." But I wasn't sure I meant it.

Ma looked me right in the eye. "Your pa isn't sure he wants to stick it out. But since we don't have the cash to start something new, maybe he'll have to." This was the first time she had talked to me this way.

"We might have to sell the milk cow," Ma went on. "Even then, I'm not sure how we'll manage."

I nearly let the bucket slide back into the well. "Sell Lissie? But . . . we couldn't!" We'd had Lissie since she was a calf. She was practically part of the family. Besides, how could we get by without milk or butter?

"I don't know for sure," Ma said. "It depends on what we

get for the corn, and *that* partly depends on whether we get some rain to plump out the kernels. But we'll need to hire people to help us harvest, and we can't go through another winter without money for coal and animal feed . . ."

I turned away, feeling sick to my stomach. I pictured the Nyberg kids after their cow died, big eyes in thin faces. My little brothers could never look like that.

That night, after Emmeline fell asleep—with her back to me again—I lit a candle then unfolded a paper bag I found in a cabinet. It was wrinkly, but it would have to do, since I couldn't find any writing paper in the house.

"Why are you girls wasting a candle?" Ma called from the other side of the curtain.

"I'll be done in a minute," I answered. I took out a stubby pencil and wrote quickly, smoothing the bag on the floor:

Housemaid For Hire
Hard worker, good at cleaning
(and can mend)
Ask for Catherine at the Potts claim or the post office

I folded the bag, put it in my dress pocket, and blew out the candle. Whether I'd have the gumption to do anything with my advertisement was another matter. But at least I could sleep tonight.

Chapter 31

The next morning, Pa said he'd take me to Ashford Manor to get my back pay and my things. Except for the outer reaches of h-e-l-l, there was no place I wanted to go less, but I couldn't say no.

We took off after breakfast. Half past seven in the morning, and it was as hot as a bread oven. The sun seemed to beat down like actual flames, and you could almost hear the prairie grass crinkling to dry, brown wisps. Only the sunflowers blooming along the side of the road seemed to like the heat, turning their bright faces toward the sky.

The folded bag in my pocket rubbed against me like a burr. Last night, writing my advertisement had seemed like the right thing to do, but now I wasn't so sure. How could I put on another black dress, sit inside and hem napkins, be called "Polly" again?

"Look," Pa said, interrupting my conversation with myself. He pointed to a brown smudge in the sky, like a dirty streak on a blue plate. "Prairie fire."

I had seen a prairie fire once, speeding flames gobbling up dry grass like demon grasshoppers. This one was far off, but it only took a lightning strike or an untended fire to start a new one.

"What if a prairie fire comes our way? Is our firebreak wide enough?" I asked Pa.

"I think so," he said. "I hope so."

The closer we got to Ashford Manor, the more I wished we were going in the other direction. The wagon rumbled past the coal shed where Eli and I had hidden, past the Prince Albert train station, past the stone English church, through the fields of wheat stubble, and up the slope toward the stable and the house. "You can stop here, Pa," I croaked when we got to the stable.

"Well, I'll be a hard-boiled egg," Pa said, staring wide-eyed from the stable to the manor. I remembered my first day, how *I* had stared, how small and frightened I had felt. My heart hammered even harder today, if that was possible.

Eli hurried out of the stable, jamming his cap onto his head. "Good morning, Mr. Potts, Cabby. May I unhitch your horses?" He flashed me a quick, sympathetic grin, which only made my heart hammer more.

"It's all right, we won't be here long," Pa said.

Eli came around to my side and put out his hand. I took it, feeling a blush creep up my neck. "What's going on?" he whispered as he helped me down. "Mrs. Shaw said you got fired. Is that true?"

"Yeah, it's true," I mumbled. There was more I wanted to say: *Yes, I was fired, and here's why. Thank you for helping me get home on the train. I miss you, Eli Lewis.* But Eli still held my hand in his strong fingers, throwing my brain into confusion.

"Why don't you go on in, Cabby?" Pa said from the

176

wagon seat. Good gracious, did he see me hand-in-hand with a *boy?*

I yanked my hand away from Eli's. "Uh, okay, Pa."

Eli stood there for a second, the grin fading from his face. "Watering trough is next to the stable, Mr. Potts." He walked away without looking back.

Stupid Cabby, look what you've done. Say something to him! But I couldn't think of a thing to say, and I had to march to Ashford Manor—the back door, of course—alone.

Mr. and Mrs. Shaw were both at the kitchen table. Something seemed strange about the scene, but I was too discombobulated to figure what it was.

"Why, it's Cabby!" said Mrs. Shaw.

"The Master says you got yourself fired," Mr. Shaw said, shaking his head mournfully. "Insolence, lass? Unbecoming behavior?"

I swallowed. There was no good way to explain. "I guess it's true. Mr. Ashford wanted us to give up our land to him, and it made me mad, so . . . I was rude, I guess." This was the truth, if not the whole truth.

"Why would Mr. Ashford care about *your* land?" Mrs. Shaw said.

"I'm trying to figure that out myself. He offered us money to relinquish our claim."

"It'll be something to do with that slick fellow, what's-'is-name Mortify," Mr. Shaw said.

"Mortimer," I said. "Mr. H. H."

"Ah," said Mrs. Shaw. "Well, never mind about that now. We're right sorry you were let go. You—well, I've 'ad worse 'ousemaids."

I couldn't help smiling. "You've had better, too, I reckon." I was going to miss Mrs. Shaw, strangely enough. She was quick to bark, but there was no bite in her. And I'd never met anyone who worked as hard.

Wait a minute . . . Mr. and Mrs. Shaw hadn't done a stitch of work since I walked in. The stove wasn't even lit. That's what seemed so strange. "It's quiet around here," I said. "Is Lady Ashford away?" That would be a relief.

Mr. and Mrs. Shaw looked at each other. "Milady's gone back to England," Mr. Shaw said. "Sophie too, naturally. They'll be underway still."

"Oh!" I said. "Why?"

As soon as the question was out of my mouth, I knew the answer. I'd seen myself how Lady Ashford was sinking down. The Prairie Cure hadn't worked.

"It'll be a wonder if she survives the journey," Mr. Shaw said softly. For once, it seemed like he was stating a fact, not being gloomy.

"I'm sorry," I said. And I was.

Mrs. Shaw sighed. "She was—is—an exacting woman, but true as the day is long, and kind to 'er servants."

"Kind?" Even now, I felt the throb of the word "superior" on my heart.

Mrs. Shaw shook her head. "Why do you think she's kept Sophie on? Another mistress would 'ave fired that woman long ago, but Milady knows she's got nowhere else to go."

I thought about that as I went up the stairs. I still wasn't convinced Lady Ashford was *kind*. But she certainly was *true*. There was no pretending with the

Ladyship, unlike with Nigel, who acted nice but was really a rat.

I forgive you, Lady Ashford, I whispered—not that she'd asked my forgiveness. I imagined her sitting upright in some dirty, jolting train car, frowning at the noise and unrefined language, and the picture hit me in the heart.

Godspeed, Milady.

Upstairs in my little bedroom, I looked one more time for my brooch, behind the bed and under the rug, but it wasn't there. I packed up the rest of my things, tempted to stick out my tongue at the hideous black dress on the hook. Instead, I held it out in front of me. It was for someone else now. *Tell them your name,* I said to the girl who'd come after me. *It gets easier when they call you by name.* I spread the dress on the bed and went downstairs.

"'Ere's your back pay, Cabby," Mrs. Shaw said, handing me some folded bills. She smooshed me into a hug.

Mr. Shaw pinched me on the cheek. "You'll come to no good, I imagine," he said—but I knew he was teasing.

I started out the door then turned back. "Something I was wondering. What is prima-primogeniture?"

"Goodness, wot put that in your 'ead?" Mrs. Shaw said.

"I don't know," I said, which was true.

"Well, in England, primogeniture means the oldest son inherits the title and the estate. No dividing up, you understand? In the Ashford case, it all goes to Edgar, without much left over for Nigel and the others. That's why Nigel's come out 'ere, other younger sons too, land being cheap in America."

I could hardly believe it. "So . . . Mr. Ashford won't be rich after all?"

"Well, rich compared to you 'n me. But not compared to 'is father."

Why hadn't I figured this out earlier? The hints were there: Nigel being so worried about his remittances, the "swarming manhood" problem, as Edwin put it . . . which meant the younger sons problem, I realized now.

"So *that's* why he's marrying Lavinia—Miss Peacock? For her money?" I said.

"Aren't you an inquisitive thing! In fact, Nigel is *not* marrying Miss Peacock. 'E asked 'er, but she turned 'im down. She's engaged to the son of some Marquess. The fellow's not as young as 'e once was, but 'e's an *only* son, and she shall be *Lady* Lavinia."

Well, knock me down with a feather. "How do you know all this?"

Mrs. Shaw chuckled. "All servants eavesdrop, Cabby. But we don't all get caught."

So Lavinia had turned Nigel down. She wanted a title, and she found a better one than wife of an Honorable. When it came to marriage, that girl was more practical than I thought.

Nigel was more practical than I thought, too. Of course he didn't like Lavinia. Maybe he actually liked my sister. I mean, who wouldn't? But he wanted a rich wife. It was all about arithmetic.

Just like it was for me. All about arithmetic. I didn't like Nigel, but I wanted a rich brother-in-law—to get me out of a job I hated, as much as anything else. Was I no better than Nigel Ashford?

I stood with my hand on the doorframe, heavy with shame. I *had* gotten out of my job, but my selfish scheme had hurt my sister and cost my family two dollars a week.

"One more thing," I said slowly, pulling the advertisement out of my pocket. "Could you take this?"

"What is it, lass?" Mrs. Shaw said.

I couldn't bear to explain, but Mrs. Shaw would know what I wanted. I pressed the folded paper bag into her hand and hurried out the door.

Chapter 32

"Were they rough on you in there, chickee?" Pa asked as we drove away.

"What? No," I murmured. "Here's my pay." I reached over and tucked the money into his pocket, all the while picturing Mrs. Shaw unfolding my advertisement, handing it to Mr. Shaw. "I guess you can take this round to the Banisters and Thistlewaites," she might be saying. How much longer 'til I was trudging up polished stairs and emptying stinking chamber pots?

We had just passed the Prince Albert station when I saw a familiar buggy rolling toward us, a slim shape on the seat. Oh great. Pa muttered something under his breath, but he pulled back on the reins anyway. It was kind of a rule on the prairie: when you met another wagon on the trail, you stopped to say howdy, no matter who it was.

When he saw us, Nigel flicked his buggy whip at Georgiana, and she took off running, charging straight toward us. At the last second, Nigel swung her out into the grass, flushing a prairie chicken from its nest. The buggy bounced to stop. "Good day to you!" Nigel shouted. His words were friendly, but I knew he was mocking us and our poky plow horses. "Were you looking for me, Mr.

Potts? Changed your mind about the land?"

"No, my girl just needed her things." Pa's voice was mild as milk, but he gripped the reins hard.

Nigel's eyes narrowed. He leaned back in the buggy seat, a thin smile on his face. "Your neighbors saw things differently, you know. The Shybergs, is it?"

"Nybergs," Pa said. "Did they . . .?"

"They were wise enough to do business with me," Nigel said.

Was this true? If so, it wasn't just for meanness that Nigel wanted our land. He wanted ours, and other people's too.

"I expect you'll regret your decision, my man," Nigel said, his voice low and hard. He smacked poor Georgiana with the whip, and the buggy sped away.

I looked over at Pa, shaky as a mouse that just escaped the cat. "What did he mean, you'll regret your decision?"

Pa clucked at the horses. "Nothing, I imagine. Those rich fellows don't like to lose, is all."

"Do you think the Nybergs really gave up their claim?"

"I don't know, Cabby. But do you want to hear something more cheerful? I met a couple of drummers in Slocum City the other day. Drummers in town means people are moving out here to Kansas." He sounded happy, excited even.

"What are drummers?"

"Travelling salesmen," Pa said. "One of them, if you can believe it, sells parlor organs."

"How does he do that? Isn't an organ awful heavy?"

Pa's eyes twinkled. "He carries a sample case, with pictures and so on. The other fellow sells all kinds of patent medicine. I almost bought Ma some Spencer's Liver Regulator, only . . ."

Only we didn't have any money to speak of. Pa didn't have to say it.

We drove on without talking much. Pa seemed distracted, whistling to himself and fiddling with the reins. When we were almost home, he said, "This was a long trip for Lightning and Bolt. Try to rest them tomorrow."

That was a curious thing to say. Why tell *me* what to do with the horses?

Then he leaned over in the wagon seat to give me a hug, which was also curious, considering how sweaty we both were.

The next morning, I understood.

I was the first to see the note on the table:

My dear wife and beloved children, I'm sorry to slip out like this but must strike while the iron is hot. I shall miss my dear chickees but will try to be back for corn harvest.
Your loving husband and father,
Albert Potts
P.S. I have taken money for the train.

I read the note over and over, the words making a cold place in my heart. When Ma came in, I handed her the note without a word. She read it then leaned against the table like she was dizzy.

"What is it, Ma?" Emmeline said.

Ma picked up a folded brochure that was propped against a bowl. I looked over her shoulder as she slowly read it aloud.

Sales Agents Wanted

*$3 Watches, Cheapest and Best in the Known World
Make up to $10 a Day!!
Don't miss this Dazzling Opportunity*

"I'd like to skin the rascal who gave him this," Ma muttered.

"It was some drummers, I guess," I said. "Pa told me he met them." I remembered Pa's eager look, the excitement in his voice. It hadn't occurred to me to tell Ma about this—or about giving Pa my pay. Now he was gone, and so was that money.

"Why did Pa go? Don't he love us any more?" Jesse said.

"*Doesn't*, Jesse," Ma corrected automatically.

"Of course he loves us," Emmeline said. "He's just going to make some money." But her voice was full of tears.

"Ten dollars a day?" Orin said. "Gee whillikers!"

"*Up to* ten dollars a day," I said, turning on him fiercely.

I don't know why I was mad at Orin. The words made my heart leap, too. *Ten dollars a day.* Even if he made half that amount, one tenth that amount. . .

Something is bound to turn up, Pa was always saying. Was this the something? Maybe Pa would sell enough three-dollar watches to solve our money problems. Then he'd come back. Once we got through the winter, it wouldn't be long before we could prove up on our claim. Then we'd own this land ourselves. One hundred and sixty acres, all ours, free and clear—and I wouldn't have to be a housemaid again.

But Pa had tried things like this before. Black's Special Tonic hadn't worked out, nor the salt well in Slippery Rock. The look on Ma's face echoed the doubt in my thorn-pricked heart.

Chapter 33

"Well, no sense sitting around," Ma said, dropping the brochure on the table. "Orin, get the stove started. Em, you make the porridge. Cabby, you can help your sister in the post office today." She was trying to make it seem like a normal day, but it wasn't, not with five places around the table instead of six.

"I almost forgot," I said after breakfast. "Pa said to rest the horses today. We need to walk to town." Tears slid down my cheeks, and I brushed them away angrily.

"All right—get a move on, then," Ma said. "I'll come to town with you girls. Mrs. Wattles said she wanted some more laying hens, and I guess I'll sell her a couple of mine. Boys, you can stay here. Jesse, make sure you mind Orin."

Ma's voice sounded strange, sort of hollow. I felt a pang as I watched her pick up a sack and head out the door. She was fond of her hens, I knew. It wasn't just the eggs. If she was selling some, she didn't believe Pa was going to make ten dollars a day, or any money at all.

The walk to town was hot and dusty and mostly quiet, except for the confused *buck-buck-buck* of the chickens in the bag Ma carried over her shoulder. Just outside town, we sat down at the edge of the road to put our shoes on. We always wore shoes in town, of course, but there was no point wasting shoe leather walking there.

We were tying our shoelaces when a rider on horseback pulled up in front of us. "Why, Mrs. Potts," said a familiar voice, "what an *opportune* meeting." It was Mr. H. H. Mortimer, his black hat resting on slick black hair, his bow tie crisply tied. I felt a chill, and not just because his horse blocked the sun.

Ma finished her laces and stood up slowly. "How can I help you, Mr. Mortimer?" I wondered if he could hear the dislike in her voice.

"I wonder if you could direct me to *Mister* Potts."

"He's gone—" Emmeline began.

"Gone on a short trip . . . for some supplies," Ma said. "I don't know exactly when he'll be back."

"In that case, I'd like to speak to *you,* dear lady," Mr. Mortimer purred. "It's a matter of some urgency," he added when Ma hesitated.

"Very well," Ma said. Mr. Mortimer wheeled his horse around, and Ma followed him, her chickens' heads poking out of the sack. I scrambled to my feet and looked after her, uneasiness flapping in my stomach.

Emmeline and I went on to the post office, and it should have been fun, sorting mail with my sister for the first time since that fateful day in June. But she was quiet and distracted—thinking about the aspersions folks might cast, I guessed. I couldn't stop worrying about what was happening in the land office.

"Has Bub Skyler gotten any more letters lately?"

I asked, trying to feel interest in Bub's long-distance romance.

"Oh yes, lots," Emmeline said with a sigh. She chewed on her little finger, a habit she had supposedly given up. "Actually, the young lady is arriving any day now."

"Oh . . . that's nice," I said. Was Ma still with Mr. Mortimer? What were they talking about? I picked up Mr. Hanley's copy of *Prairie Farmer,* but I couldn't focus on an article about feeding sweet potatoes to your hog. Not that we had a hog anyway.

Finally I couldn't stand it any longer. "I've got to see what's happening." Before Emmeline could protest, I slipped out of the post office, weaved through the people in the store, and hurried into the street. I was running full speed by the time I got to the land office.

I almost collided with Ma coming out. She looked like a different person: bent over like a heavy grass stem, her eyes dark hollows in her pale face. The chickens in her bag were silent, and I had the crazy fear that being with Mr. Mortimer had killed them. "What is it, Ma? What happened?" I breathed.

Ma drifted to the bench in front of the former Prouty Boarding House and sat down. "One hundred and sixty acres for eighteen dollars," she murmured, talking to herself more than to me. "I should have known it was too good to be true."

I was ready to jump out of my skin. "Ma! What's going on?"

She stared at me with a strange, flat look. "Mr. Mortimer says our claim belongs to someone else."

Her words made no sense. I just shook my head.

"He says we have to move off our land."

"No we don't," I said. This was contradicting, but I couldn't help it. "Pa told Mr. Ashford no, remember?"

"It's not Mr. Ashford." She gestured vaguely into the distance. "According to Mr. Mortimer, a Mr. *Myers* filed a claim on our quarter-section ten years ago, then paid cash to get title to the land. He went out West but now wishes to return to his land. Mr. Mortimer showed me the title."

I could barely make sense of her words. "But that's impossible. *We* filed claim on that section."

Ma said nothing.

"It's a lie!" I shouted. The hens in Ma's sack clucked in alarm—at least they were alive.

"It's got to be a fake, that title," I said more quietly.

"Maybe it is," Ma said. She still had that strange, flat look. "Mr. Mortimer said we were welcome to contest it."

"Oh," I said with a rush of relief. "Why didn't you say so?" I sank onto the bench beside her.

"Contesting a claim costs fifty dollars," Ma said. She started to laugh. "Fifty dollars!" She laughed so hard tears rolled out of the corners of her eyes.

Her laughing scared me. "What are we supposed to do?" I said, just to get her to stop.

Ma swiped at her eyes with her sleeve. "Who knows? Hope we find money under our mattresses? File another claim? Though Mr. Mortimer says most of the sections around here are taken."

It was too much. How could we have lost our land? And how could Pa have left us at the very time we needed him? I sagged against the rough boards behind me, dully repeating Ma's words in my mind: *move off our land . . . showed me the title . . . not Mr. Ashford . . . not Mr. Ashford . . .*

Then I remembered Nigel's cold words: *You* will *accept my offer . . . I expect you'll regret your decision, my man . . .*

"Wait a minute!" I choked, tugging at Ma's sleeve. "It *is* Mr. Ashford. It has to be!"

Chapter 34

Ma looked at me without much interest. "Oh?"

I jumped to my feet. "It's *Nigel* who wants our land! This is some kind of trick. We have to go back to Mr. Mortimer, make him admit it!"

"Hush, Cabby," Ma said. "I am not going back to Mr. Mortimer."

I wanted to shake her. I wanted to rush into Mr. H. H. Mortimer's office and throttle him with his bow tie. Instead, I grabbed hold of myself and took a breath. "Ma, just this once, don't 'hush-Cabby' me."

Startled, she looked me in the eye.

"I know I have a big mouth, I know I'm hasty and forward, like you say. But I want to hang onto our land as much as you do . . ."

"I know that," Ma said wearily.

"Let me hear what Mr. Mortimer has to say, and maybe I'll have an idea."

Ma looked me up and down for a long minute, like she was measuring me for a dress. Finally she nodded. "Well, all right. *I'll* talk to Mr. Mortimer again. You can come, but don't make a scene. Do you understand?"

Two minutes later, Ma and I sat across from Mr. H. H. Mortimer in the land office, Ma's chicken sack on her lap.

Notices on the wall looked down at us. *Choice Government Land,* said one. *Luxurious Grasses, Fertile Soil, All you Need for Wealth and Comfort,* said another.

"My dear Mrs. Potts," Mr. Mortimer said, "I hadn't expected to see you again so soon. And you've brought your daughter," he added with an unfriendly smile.

I was so nervous I had to put my hand on my knee to keep it from shaking. There was something about Mr. Mortimer—"that slick fellow, what's-'is-name Mortify," Mr. Shaw had called him—that quenched my courage like cold water on a match.

"Perhaps," Ma said, "we could see that title one more time?"

"Why, of course," Mr. Mortimer smiled. He pulled a piece of paper from a stack on his desk.

I looked at it stupidly. It had fancy letters and fancy words: *hereby certified . . . payment in full . . . Thomas Thurston Myers.* How did I know this was a fake?

"Well, if that will be all . . ." Mr. Mortimer pushed his chair back.

There had to be something I was missing. If Nigel was behind this, *why* did he want our claim—and the Nybergs'? That was the piece of the puzzle I still couldn't figure out.

Think, Cabby.

I pictured myself scritch-scratching with my scrub brush, pictured Nigel, Sir Roger, and Mr. Mortimer leaning over a map in the drawing room. "People will be flocking to Kansas, all wanting farmland," Sir Roger had said. "All needing to buy it from the Honorable Nigel Ashford."

All needing to buy it from Nigel. Yes, that was it. I had been thinking about this the wrong way. It wasn't that Nigel wanted *our* land—not ours in particular, that is. He wanted *all* the land around here. If he owned it all, he could set whatever price he wanted, put up fences, or turn it all into cattle land.

"But a lot of the land around here is owned by Uncle Sam," Nigel had objected. "There are rules, are there not?"

"That's where a friendly land agent comes in," Sir Roger had said.

Those scoundrels! I took a breath, my courage re-lit.

"May I see the map, please?" I said, in the meekest voice I could come up with. "The, uh, county map, with all the land around here. Maybe there's another section we could file a claim on."

Mr. Mortimer's smile wobbled. "Why don't you leave that to your father, young lady? Now, if you'll excuse me . . ."

Ma leaned toward him. "My daughter would like to see the map." There was a growl in her voice, like Snuff's when he caught the scent of coyote.

Mr. Mortimer glanced at her, hesitated, then spread a map in front of us. "If you insist," he said lightly.

It was funny how in Kansas the roads and wagon trails ran all higgledy-piggledy, but the map made it look like everything was in neat squares. There was Slocum City, with the town lots lined up on either side of the railroad tracks. Outside the city were square-mile sections cut up into quarter-sections like ours. I saw our quarter-section, with "Potts" crossed off and "Myers" written above it. The Nybergs' quarter-section also had the name crossed off.

All the other sections around ours and the Nybergs, the ones I thought were empty, had names written in them too. Every single one. "Smith," "Jones," "Martin," "Matthews," and so on, all in Mr. H. H. Mortimer's careful handwriting.

I looked up. "Oh my, that's a lot of new claims. Who are all these people?" I asked, harmless as a wobbly-leg lamb.

"Why, they're new homesteaders," Mr. Mortimer said, like he was talking to a child.

"New homesteaders?" I repeated. "I don't actually remember seeing any new folks around town—I mean, don't you have to be *present* to homestead?" I bit my lip, trying to look innocent.

Mr. Mortimer waved his hand airily. "There's no rule requiring homesteaders to make their whereabouts known to *you,* my dear." He chuckled like he'd made a joke, and I felt my blood start to boil. How dare he?

I jumped to my feet. "These names aren't real, are they?" I demanded. "Even Mr. Myers! There are no new homesteaders. It's *Mr. Ashford* who wants—"

Mr. Mortimer stood up suddenly. He looked calm, but he was blinking fast. He slid the map under some other papers. "Excuse me, I have a *very* busy day . . ."

Tarnation! I had made a scene after all, and now he was spooked.

Ma stood up too, slinging her bag over her shoulder. "We do thank you for your time, Mr. Mortimer. You've been most helpful." She hurried out of the office, and I followed.

"I'm sorry, Ma," I said when we were out in the street. "I didn't mean to shout at him . . ."

"It's all right, Cabby," she said calmly. She strode along energetically, and I could barely keep up. "I think you're right. I've heard of this kind of thing before. I'll wager those names are dummy applications, and the real name on every square of that map is Nigel Ashford. I don't know why I didn't see it before."

"Okay . . . Where are you going?" I panted.

Ma laughed and stopped walking. "I think better when I walk, I guess. Now, I have to see about these hens. Then I want to talk to Mr. Meacham. He meets most everybody who comes through town, and if he hasn't seen any Mr. 'Myers,' or 'Smith,' or 'Jones,' then we'll know we're right. Don't know what we'll do about it, but at least we'll know what's going on."

It was a serious situation, but I couldn't help smiling. Ma said "we." Her and me. Ma and Cabby. For the first time in maybe my whole life, I felt like my mother and I were partners.

"You go help Emmeline finish in the post office. When you're done, you girls can head on home."

I nodded, hurried down the street, pushed open the door of Nehemiah Meacham's General Store and Post Office, and walked straight into a *situation*.

Chapter 35

In the store, people crowded around a man and a young lady. The lady was a stranger, a short curly-haired woman in a rumpled dress and sooty white gloves, a scuffed, dented trunk beside her. The man at her side was Bub Skyler. He wore trousers instead of overalls, a cleanish shirt, and a grin as wide as a river.

"What's going on?" I whispered to Adelaide Buchanan, who stood near the door.

"Can you believe it?" she whispered back. "Miss O'Donovan came all the way from New York to marry Bub Skyler!"

"So she's really here!" I said.

"You knew about this?" Adelaide said.

"Sort of . . ."

A harsh voice cut through the murmurs. "Bridget O'Donovan? What kind of name is that?"

It was Mrs. Snopes. I could just see the top of her black bonnet, the stuffed bird practically hopping with excitement.

The lady—Bridget—stared at Mrs. Snopes, hands on her hips. "My *name's* Irish. But I'm an *American*." I could tell I was going to like her.

"Huh," Mrs. Snopes grunted. "I'll bet you're a Catholic,

though. Bub Skyler, I call this a disgrace!"

Emmeline, I could see through the crowd, was leaning over the top half of the post office door, her face flushed. "Mrs. Snopes," she called, "what does it matter if Bridget's a Catholic? Don't you think we ought to welcome her to Slocum City?"

Mrs. Snopes wheeled on my sister. "What do *you* know about what's proper? I saw you throw yourself at that Englishman!"

People turned to stare at Emmeline. I stepped forward, my fists clenched. Could I punch Mrs. Snopes in the nose?

"Carrying on about how he ought to love you!" Mrs. Snopes spat. "I say you've besmirched the reputation of—ooh!"

Knee-High Meacham appeared behind Mrs. Snopes and suddenly, unbelievably, *picked her up*. I nearly collapsed with shock.

Holding Mrs. Snopes against his side like a rag doll, Knee-High swept aside some boxes on a top shelf. Then he lifted the little woman and sat her on the shelf.

"Nehemiah—help—no—put me down!" Mrs. Snopes sputtered. But she didn't dare kick, for fear of falling. She couldn't jump, because it was too high. There she sat like a bolt of cloth, her little button-up boots dangling, while some folks gasped and some started to laugh.

"Now you listen to me, Mrs. Snopes!" Knee-High commanded. He didn't stammer one bit. "First of all, it's no business of yours what flavor of Christian Miss O'Donovan is."

"That's right!" said Bub Skyler. He put his thick arm

around Bridget's waist.

"Hey, we ain't married yet, Bub!" she said, swatting him away. Everybody laughed.

"Furthermore," Knee-High went on, "you've no right to say anything against Miss Emmeline P-P-P . . ." Suddenly, his stammer returned. "P-Potts," he pronounced at last. "If anyone was at fault in this business, it was that A-Ashford fellow. Em-Em-Emmeline is . . . is . . ."

"She is the most kind-hearted person I know!" said Mrs. Nyberg from the crowd. "Just the other day, she slipped me three cents for a stamp."

"What's this fuss all about?" bellowed old Dr. Wattles, who was almost deaf. "Has anybody got anything to say against our Emmeline?"

My sister put her hand to her throat. "Thank you," she gulped, looking at Knee-High with shining eyes.

Just then, *Mr.* Snopes rushed into the store with his barber's apron still on. "Lucretia, oh my goodness, come down from there at once," he squeaked. This made everybody laugh again, which made Mrs. Snopes so mad she started babbling like a lunatic. "Never in my born days—this is intoler—put me—aah!"

"Before I get you down, I want you to apologize to Bridget and Em-Em-Emmeline," Knee-High said, "and . . ."

I stepped into the middle of the store. "And promise to stop judging people all the time," I said firmly, glaring up at Mrs. Snopes on her shelf.

"Yeah!" a lot of folks agreed.

"I guess you'd better do it, Lucretia," Mr. Snopes said.

"Fine! I'm sorry and I promise," Mrs. Snopes said. She didn't sound sincere, but at least she said it.

Knee-High set Mrs. Snopes down as gently as possible, and she and her husband scuttled out. Everyone started talking excitedly. Meanwhile, Emmeline looked at Knee-High, her cheeks pink. He looked back at her and turned scarlet. It was amazing their hot faces didn't start a fire.

"Hey, Mr. Meacham, can I buy some nails?" someone said, and the situation was over.

"Did you see her swing those little shoes?" I cackled on our way home.

"She—looked—so—funny," Emmeline gasped. We both laughed so hard we almost fell over. The birds perched on the grass stems must have thought we were crazy.

I hadn't forgotten our problems, hadn't forgotten that Mr. H. H. Mortimer said we had to leave our land, or that Pa was gone. But it was good to laugh with my sister, good to have my best friend back. I would wait until we got home to tell her about Mr. Mortimer and Nigel's scheme, in case it made her start languishing again.

"Seriously, Knee-High was heroic, don't you think?" I said when I couldn't laugh any more.

"Mmm." Emmeline suddenly seemed to find her sunbonnet strings very interesting. "Yes, I guess so."

That was an odd answer. I looked at my sister curiously. Did she know what I knew, that Knee-High Meacham was in love with her?

"Oh!" she said, reaching into her pocket. "I forgot to give you this." She handed me a letter.

If she was trying to change the subject, she did a good job. I snatched the envelope, my heart going *thud, thud* in my chest. Could it be from Eli?

"Cabby, you're blushing! Do you have a *sweetheart?*"

"No!" Of course it wasn't Eli. Why would he write to the girl who had brushed off his hand, who had never thanked him for helping her? And why did Emmeline think I was blushing? I certainly was not.

Now I recognized the squarish handwriting.

"It's only from Mrs. Shaw," I muttered. I turned away from Emmeline and ripped the envelope open.

Dear Cabby,

I write in haste as I have just run into Lady Banister in Prince Albert. She says her housemaid has up and quit and normally she wouldn't want to hire a servant as was let go but seeing as how I gave you a good character she would in this case and you should apply in person at Ironwood Manor, as their place is called.

Mrs. Shaw

It took me a minute to untangle Mrs. Shaw's grammar, but soon enough the meaning was clear. I stood in the road, holding the letter in my fingertips. How easy it would be to loosen my fingers, let the wind carry it off until it was just a speck in the distance. Instead, I handed the letter to Emmeline, and she read it quickly.

"Cabby," she gasped, "why does she say this? Why would you work for *Lady Banister?*"

"Do you remember her?"

"Of course. She looked at us like we were animals in a zoo. Why would Mrs. Shaw . . .?"

"I kind of asked her to find me another job," I said

miserably.

"But you don't have to take it, do you? Listen, you don't even have to tell Ma about this." Emmeline linked her arm in mine.

I was glad my sister was on my side. But she didn't know the whole story. I pictured the title Mr. Mortimer had shown us. *Hereby certified . . . paid in full.* Even if it was a fake, even if there was no Mr. Myers, what would stop Nigel and Mr. Mortimer from sending the sheriff after us? Fifty dollars might stop them, if we filed to contest the claim . . . The truth was, we needed money now more than ever.

On the other hand . . . Lady Banister.

When we got home, I put the letter from Mrs. Shaw under my pillow. I would tell Ma about it soon. Really, I would.

Chapter 36

"Cabby, don't pull the thread so tight," Ma chided the next night, frowning at me over her knitting needles. "You're darning a sock, not playing tug o' war."

I sighed. Mending still made me itch with impatience. Besides, it seemed to me we had more urgent things to think about than worn-out socks.

Just then, there was a knock at the door. "Is it Pa?" I breathed. I couldn't believe how much I wanted it to be him. It would just make everyone more hopeful.

Orin hurried to open the door, but the big man standing there wasn't Pa. It was Knee-High Meacham— or rather, a younger version of Knee-High, someone with clean-shaven cheeks, deep-set brown eyes, and a shy smile.

Emmeline looked up, then immediately looked down at her mending.

"Why, Nehemiah, come in. Won't you sit down?" Ma said.

Nehemiah was Knee-High's real name. So it *was* him, but without his whiskers. He ducked through the doorway and stood twisting his hat in his hands until I was sure he'd shred it to bits. When Ma pointed to a chair, he sat down gingerly, his hat still in his hands.

"Mrs. Potts," Knee-High said, looking only at Ma. "I wanted t-to tell you I spoke with some of the men." He stopped and took a breath. "None of us have seen any Myers or Smith or Jones in town, and we think all those applications are fake. The m-m-men agreed to have a meeting next Tuesday to talk about the situation. I'm sure we can get Mr. Mortimer there—ask him to give a speech, or something—but I'm not sure about Mr. A-Ash . . . that other fellow."

"A *meeting?*" Orin said. "I think we should just go *pound* Mr. Mortimer. Mr. Ashford too."

I didn't say it, but I sort of agreed with Orin. Still, a meeting might be useful. "I could explain to everybody how I heard Nigel and Sir Roger and Mr. Mortimer cooking up their land-grabbing scheme," I said. It made me nervous to think about speaking in front of a crowd, but I reckoned I could do it.

Knee-High cleared his throat. "It's only g-g-going to be men. Except for your mother, since Mr. P-Potts is travelling."

"My pa is *drumming,*" Jesse said. "Only he hasn't got a drum." Jesse found this very disappointing.

Men only? Of all the confounded, old-fashioned ideas.

Meanwhile Knee-High started worrying at his hat again, round and round in his big hands. Then he stood up so suddenly he knocked his chair over. He leaned over to pick up the chair and knocked a basin off a shelf. When he had picked up the chair and the basin, he straightened, his face red. "E-Emmeline, I wonder if we could t-talk outside, j-just for a moment."

Emmeline stood up too, her mending falling from her lap, and followed Knee-High out the door without a word.

This was an interesting development, but I was so peeved I didn't care right then. I folded my arms. "Ma, I don't see why I can't come to the meeting. I mean, I'm the one who figured out . . ."

"I know, Cabby," Ma said. "I'm sorry, but that's just the way things are." She smiled at me, and I felt it again, that me-and-Ma-are-partners thing. It made me feel a little better, actually.

I went to the window, standing to the side so Emmeline and Knee-High wouldn't see me spying. Amazingly, Ma stood behind me, while the boys played at the table, oblivious to the drama unfolding outside.

Knee-High and my sister stood facing each other across Knee-High's rickety mule cart. They were talking softly, and even in the twilight I could see how tenderly he looked at her. The mule let out a *hee-haw-haw-haw* like the creaking of a giant door hinge. Knee-High scratched the shaggy creature between her ears and grinned down at Emmeline, who smiled back.

This wasn't exactly poetry, but somehow it was the most beautiful thing I had seen in a long time. I was almost ready to cry.

Nigel Ashford had told the truth about one thing, I realized: this "big oaf of a shopkeeper," as Nigel had called him, loved my sister. And he was a thousand times more worthy of her, even if he was poor. Some things mattered more than arithmetic. Even I could see that now.

Knee-High put out his hand to help her into the cart. She hesitated, twisting her fingers together.

Do it, Em, I urged silently. *Take his hand.*

At that moment Ma touched my shoulder. "That's enough spying, Cabby." I think she was afraid I'd see a kiss. Reluctantly, I sat down and picked up my darning egg.

Just a minute later, Emmeline came inside, biting her lip and blinking hard. She refused to answer questions. It wasn't until late that night, when Ma was asleep, that she turned to me and whispered, "Do you think I'm a terrible person?"

"Of course not," I whispered back. "What are you talking about?"

"He—Knee-High—asked me to take a ride with him. He thought we could get to know each other." She sniffed, and I heard tears plop onto her pillow. "And I said no."

"Are you crazy?" I remembered another late-night conversation, when we had laughed at the idea of Emmeline marrying Knee-High. I felt bad about that now. "You like him, don't you?"

"Yes, I do. It's just . . ."

"What?"

"A week ago, I was ready to marry Nigel Ashford. There must be something wrong with me!"

"Well," I said, trying to work this out in my mind, "if it doesn't bother Knee-High that you used to care for Nigel, why should it bother you?"

Emmeline said nothing, just cried harder.

"For goodness sake," I hissed, "you don't *still* love Nigel, do you? Even Lavinia Peacock wouldn't marry that man!"

Oops, I hadn't meant to tell her that.

"I don't care, and I *don't* still love him. How can you say that?"

"Because *you* just said—"

"Girls!" Ma called from the other side of the curtain. I guess she wasn't asleep. "Don't argue. I expect Emmeline will figure this out."

I rolled away from my sister, exasperated. *I* was never going to fall in love.

Chapter 37

The next Tuesday, my mother plus all the men of Slocum City gathered in the dining room of the Grand Paris Hotel while all the ladies and children did not. Useless and frustrated, I sat outside the hotel, kicking my heels against the bench. If only Pa was here. I bet he would let me go to the meeting.

When I couldn't endure sitting any longer, I got up and skulked down Main Street, half-listening to the conversations ladies were having on the sweltering sidewalk. Mostly, they were talking about the heat. We needed rain so badly. I wanted to talk to Mrs. Nyberg, to ask if they had really agreed to give up their claim to Nigel, but I didn't see her.

Finally I couldn't endure skulking either, so I found my sister in the post office, where she was counting the money in the till. "I'm going crazy," I said. "You have any magazines I can read?"

"Two dollars and . . . fifteen cents," Emmeline said, writing down her sum. "Sorry, all the magazines got picked up. Do you want this *Dodge City Times* newspaper? It's a year old."

It would have to do. I handed her the section with poems and stories, and I read old news. A boy had fallen in a well but had been rescued . . . Someone's horse had been stolen, along with a good saddle and bridle—"Indians traveling through the area" were blamed for this crime, naturally . . .

I almost put the paper down, but something caught my eye. "Hey!" I said. "Listen to this."

Notorious Land Agent Skips Town
Mr. J. B. Wentworth, land agent, hopped out of Dodge City on Saturday before the sheriff could lay hands on him. Mr. Wentworth, a man of oily manner and questionable character, was suspected of proving up on illegal homesteading applications. The "dwellings" on these claims proved to be nothing more than houses on wheels, conveniently moved from location to location.

Emmeline laughed. "Houses on wheels? That's creative, anyway."

"Wait a minute," I said. "'Oily manner and questionable character.' Who does that sound like?"

She stared at me.

"Listen, this paper is a year old, right?"

"Yes . . ."

"And Mr. Mortimer got here about a year ago, right?"

Emmeline took the paper and read the story again. "So you think Mr. H. H. Mortimer is really Mr. J. B. Wentworth of Dodge City? I don't know, Cabby."

"It's got to be! He hopped out of that town and hopped over here. To do the same thing—get land for speculators like Nigel, instead of real homesteaders."

"An alias . . ." she said slowly.

"It would explain why he never gets any mail."

"And why he dyes his hair. I *knew* that shiny black hair was fake." She shivered. "Imagine, a desperate fugitive, right here in Slocum City!"

"I know," I said. "We have to tell everybody, right now."

Emmeline's eyes widened. "Don't even think about it, Cabby Potts. We are *not* going into that meeting. Ma would kill us."

She was probably right about that. But if ever there was a time to disobey, this was it. I took the newspaper back. "*I'm* going, Em."

A minute later, I stood outside the dining room of the Grand Paris Hotel, my legs melting beneath me, my heart thumping in my chest. A solid wall of men's backs blocked my way into the room. *Little Girls Not Welcome* seemed to be written on the wall.

I forced myself to listen hard to what was happening in the room. Ma must have just finished what she had to say, because I heard Knee-High say, "Thank you, Mrs. P-Potts," and a bunch of men started talking at once. I caught phrases like "nerve of that Englishman!" and "land grabber!" and "have them both arrested!" Everyone sounded spitting mad, which was a good sign, I reckoned. Especially mad was a man whose voice I didn't recognize. "Me and my wife just got to town, and Mr. Mortimer said there were no more quarter-sections to be had. Can you believe it?"

Then Bub Skyler spoke up, loud and clear. "Where is that hornswoggling land agent? What's he got to say for himself?"

There was a pause, during which I found a gap and wormed my way along the side of the room, hiding behind a folded-up table. I peeked out as Mr. H. H. Mortimer got up and started talking. His voice was soothing and slick, oozing through the room like melted butter. "Gentlemen. Surely you don't believe that *I* would sign off on false titles, or approve dummy homesteading claims?" He stood facing the men, his bow tie perfectly straight, his hair perfectly combed. "Why, I am an agent of the United States government. I adhere to the rules with strict regularity."

Adhere to the rules. What a bunch of hogwash. This government agent followed only one rule: help rich folks grab up land—and get bribes in return, I reckoned.

"If you examine my paperwork," Mr. Mortimer continued, "you'll see it's all in order." The more he droned on, the more the men in the room nodded their heads. It might have been the land agent's nice suit, or his big words, or just his silky way of talking. Pretty soon Mr. H. H. Mortimer was going to talk them all 'round to his point of view, and Nigel would be on his way to owning a good-size chunk of Kansas—including our claim. He'd get it for a song and sell it for a fortune.

I had to speak up, tell everyone that H. H. Mortimer was really J. B. Wentworth, a criminal.

But what if I was wrong? What if I'd jumped to conclusions? It had certainly happened before.

And Ma would be furious, just when she was starting to trust me again . . .

I stepped out from behind the table. It had to be done. "Mr. J. B. Wentworth?" I said. But my scared voice came out tiny. No one heard me.

I swallowed hard, cleared my throat, and *shouted.* "Mr. J. B. Wentworth!"

In the split second that followed, I thought I was done for. Then Mr. Mortimer stopped talking and swiveled around to look for the voice. "Yes?"

"Cabby?" Ma gasped.

My mouth felt like it was full of cotton wool, and my knees shook so badly. But I stepped to the front of the room and climbed onto a chair. "Hey, everybody," I croaked.

"Pay no attention to this chit of a girl," Mr. Mortimer said, trying to sneer.

"What's going on, Cabby?" Bub Skyler called.

"Don't believe anything Mr. Mortimer tells you," I began, trying not to look at Ma in the front row.

"Speak up!" someone shouted.

"In fact," I said, forcing my quivery voice louder, "that man isn't H. H. Mortimer at all. He's a crook and a swindler." I pulled the newspaper page from my pocket and started to read. "Mr. J. B. Wentworth, land agent, hopped out of Dodge City . . ."

"This is balderdash!" Mr. Mortimer interrupted. "I must protest vehemently . . ." But his face had gone as pale as an unbaked pie crust.

"That conniving rascal!" Bub Skyler shouted. "Let me at him!" He elbowed his way toward the front.

Before Bub could reach Mr. Mortimer, the sound of shouts from the street filtered into the room. Everyone froze. Pounding feet echoed up the hallway. I looked over the crowd and just about fell off the chair in shock: *Eli*

Lewis was standing in the dining room doorway.

I caught his eye over the sea of faces, and we stared at each other for one quick breath. Then Eli put his hands to his mouth as a megaphone. "*Fire!*" he yelled. "Out past my ma's stable, but comin' this way fast!"

Chapter 38

The room exploded like a stepped-on ant hill. Chairs toppled, and all the men—including Mr. J. B. Wentworth, I supposed—surged for the door. Then it was only Ma and me in the empty dining room. I climbed down from my chair, afraid to look at her. But when I did look, she was smiling. "You are a bold one, Catherine Potts. Come on now, fire won't wait."

We hurried outside and joined the river of folks rushing down Main Street, past the train depot and the dry-goods store and Sawyer's Blacksmith's Shop. As we ran across the stretch of prairie between town and Mrs. Lewis's stable, I could smell smoke and hear the crackling of fire. Soon I saw flames licking through the dry grass just beyond the stable, spurting in jets that flared up and ran in lines.

"Get water!" some people shouted.

"It's too late—we can't save the building!" other people yelled.

The horses, I thought in horror, *where are the horses?* I pushed through the crowd and ran toward the stable, almost colliding with Eli as he led a pair of plow horses through the corral gate. Behind him, Mrs. Lewis led two spotted ponies.

"Take the horses, Cabby!" Eli shouted. If he was mad at me, there was no time for that now.

I gulped. The plow horses towered over me, and I didn't like the wild look in their eyes.

Knee-High appeared beside us. "I've got these big fellows—you take the ponies, Cabby. Go on, Eli, you only have a few minutes to rescue some of your ma's things."

As I grabbed the ponies' lead ropes, Mrs. Lewis took me by the shoulders. "Tie the horses in town. But if the fire comes, untie them and let them run."

"Okay," I choked.

"Not just mine, but *all the horses.* Understand?"

I nodded mutely, although Mrs. Lewis had already sprinted off. I thought of the fire sweeping through town, trapping the horses then racing across the prairie. Orin and Jesse were home alone—would the firebreak stop the flames?

Knee-High and I tied the horses to the hotel hitching rail. Just as we finished, I heard yells from the crowd. I looked back toward the stable to see flames shooting in the air, topped by thick, black smoke. "Oh, no," I groaned.

"All that hay and dry lumber—the stable had no chance," Knee-High said grimly.

I grabbed him by the arm. "Does Slocum City have a chance?" Smoke already blew up Main Street, making everything murky. "*Does it,* Knee-High?"

"Of course it does, Cabby." Knee-High pulled out of my grasp and ran off. "Let's go!" he shouted over his shoulder.

I ran to the town pump, where Bub Skyler pounded the handle up and down. As the water gushed out, people hurried up with buckets. "Make a line!" they shouted. "Hand them down!" Other people rushed up with sacks and blankets, dunking them in the trough and racing toward the fire.

I didn't have a sack or a bucket. Where were Ma and Emmeline? Where was *Pa*? Why wasn't he here to help us? Helplessly, I ran toward the flames, seeing them advance toward town like jumpy, flickering soldiers.

A burning cinder landed right at my feet. I hopped back as the grasses around me shot up in flames. In desperation, I wiggled out of my petticoat and raised it to beat at the flames.

"No, no!" squawked Mrs. Snopes.

What, worried about modesty, now?

"You have to get it wet," she croaked. Her voice was raspy, and her little hat hung sideways on her head. She batted at the fire with a dripping sack tied to a broom handle.

"Right," I panted. I ran to the trough, dunked my petticoat in the water, and rushed back to the fire, where I found Ma and Emmeline beating at the flames, their faces smudged with soot. Wordlessly, Ma pointed at a creeping line of fire.

Run, dip, swing, beat, beat, beat. Over and over and over. Every time it seemed like all the flames were out, a blowing spark would ignite a new patch of grass even closer to town. Soon I was so exhausted I could barely lift my arms, and my eyes felt raw and sore. But I didn't stop. No one did. Even old Dr. Wattles and Mrs. Wattles staggered back and forth with buckets of water. Eli and Mrs. Lewis seemed to be everywhere at once.

It went on for ages, but finally I noticed people straightening their backs or leaning on rakes or hoes. Wisps of smoke still curled here and there, but I didn't see any more flames. People kept dousing the blackened grass, bucket after bucket, but soon it was clear the fire was out. "Done. Enough," somebody said. A few people cheered, but I was too tired.

Our ragged line was just a stone's throw from Main Street.

Now that the town was safe, folks drifted toward the Lewis place. Everybody had red eyes and black-streaked faces. We looked like very tired raccoons.

One corner of Lewis Livery Stable still stood, "Fine Hor—" legible on the roof. The rest of Mrs. Lewis's stable was a charred ruin. A pile of rescued possessions sat nearby: a saddle, a few pots and pans, and a blanket or two.

I ran to Eli and gave him a hug. Who cared what folks thought about that? Emmeline hurried over and put her arm across Mrs. Lewis's drooping shoulders. "I'm so sorry, Mrs. Lewis." Other people murmured the same thing.

Maybe it was fighting the fire, everyone together. When you work shoulder to shoulder with people, maybe it's easier to remember that they're just folks.

"We'll do what we can to help you rebuild, Mrs. Lewis," said Mr. Hanley.

"That's right," echoed Mrs. Wattles. "We'll organize the collection, won't we, dear?"

"Eh? What's that?" yelled deaf Dr. Wattles.

"Mrs. Lewis can share my room at the Grand Paris

until her place is livable," said Bridget O'Donovan. "I don't mind at all."

"Why, Miss O'Donovan!" cried Mrs. Snopes. "Of all the improp—" She stopped suddenly, maybe not wanting to end up on Knee-High's shelf again, and Emmeline gave her an encouraging smile.

"I can make a shelter here," Mrs. Lewis said. "I do thank all of you, but I don't need charity." She spoke slowly and carefully, getting the English right. These might have been the most words she'd ever spoken to the people of Slocum City.

"There's another way you can help," Eli said. He looked from face to face, and I couldn't help recalling the day of the horse race, when people stared at him so hatefully. "My ma's got horses to sell. Two plow horses and two spotted ponies." If Eli recalled that day too, he didn't show it.

"I'm going to need a team," said a man whose name I didn't know, the one who said he was looking for a claim. "I'll take a look at your plow horses."

"Those spotted ponies are dandy little fellows," I found myself saying.

Everybody looked at me, and I made sure my voice was clear and strong. This time, I was going to speak up for Eli and Mrs. Lewis. "They're nimble, and they know right where you want to go, and they never step in gopher holes, even if you *happen* to take one of them for a ride across the prairie . . ."

Now I was babbling. I was too tired to feel embarrassed, though. And possibly my big mouth would do some good. I saw Bub Skyler raise an eyebrow and say "Huh," like maybe he was thinking about a Kiowa pony for his new wife. I hoped so.

Eli poked his elbow into my side. "Thanks," he muttered.

"You're welcome," I said, elbowing him back. I needed to say more, to say I was sorry for pulling away from him, thank him for helping me. But I suddenly remembered: I was standing in front of Eli Lewis with my wet, charred petticoat in my hands.

"Come, Eli," said Mrs. Lewis, "we need to get the horses."

Eli glanced at the singed petticoat and flashed me a grin. I tossed my head—I couldn't help it—and grinned back defiantly. Hopefully he knew what I'd wanted to say.

Eli followed his mother, and I caught up with Emmeline. She was at the end of the line of people trudging back toward town in the almost-dark.

As we passed the land office, I saw a shadowy figure inside. I stopped. "Hey, Em, do you think that's Mr. Mortimer—I mean Mr. Wentworth—hiding in there?"

"I don't know, and right now I don't care," she said with a yawn.

Just then, the figure stepped out of the land office doorway. It was a tall, slender farmer in overalls and a ten-gallon hat pulled low over his eyes. I remembered seeing him at the meeting and wondering who he was.

"Miss Potts?" he said.

We both jumped. This was no farmer. It was Nigel Ashford.

—Part 6—

A Gift

Chapter 39

N igel looked up and down the street and stepped closer to us. "May I have a word with you, Miss Potts?" He was wearing stiff new overalls and a crisp blue bandana tied in a knot at his neck. His hat was brand new. He looked ridiculous, like he was going to a costume party.

Emmeline shrank back. "I don't know . . ."

"Hey!" I had just noticed that Nigel's hands and face were perfectly clean, I glared at him. "Where were *you* . . .?"

"Cabby," Emmeline said warningly.

It was hard, but I closed my mouth.

"Miss Potts . . . Emmeline," Nigel said, keeping his voice low and ignoring me completely. "May I appeal to you? I fear that the citizens of this town are, er, turning against me."

I couldn't believe he thought my sister would listen to him. Nigel Ashford's opinion of himself was as puffed up as a singing bullfrog.

"This will disadvantage me," Nigel went on, leaning close to her and glancing anxiously up the street, "in any future dealings of . . . of an economic nature."

"These citizens," Emmeline said, trembling just a little, "don't they have reason for turning against you?"

"Oh, you mean the homesteading claims," Nigel said carelessly.

"*Dummy* homesteading claims," she said. "And the false title against our land." I was so proud of my sister.

Nigel touched the end of his moustache with a slim, white finger. "Any, er, irregularities were not my idea. Sir Roger and Mr. Mortimer . . ."

Emmeline folded her arms. "You're blaming others for what you did?"

"Why, Emmeline," Nigel said, putting his hand to his heart like she had stabbed him, "are you turning against me too? I am, that is, I was . . . genuinely fond of you."

"*Were you?*" Now she sounded like she might cry.

"Yes, of course," Nigel said, after what seemed like a long pause. "Of course I was." He pulled the hat off his head, ruffling his hair, and stared piteously at my sister. He looked so melancholy that I actually believed what he was saying. Anyway, how could he help being fond of Emmeline? Everyone who met her was fond of her. He had liked her, kissed her . . . and dumped her.

"You just have to understand," Nigel said, "how someone in my position has a certain lifestyle to maintain—that is, certain standards to uphold . . ."

I felt my mouth drop open. So being associated with my sister was *lowering his standards?* I realized now that Nigel would never have married Emmeline, even if he did love her. I looked at my sister, but she wasn't trembling any more. Or crying or languishing or anything.

"I understand you, Mr. Ashford," she said calmly. She even smiled. "I understand you perfectly."

"So . . ."

"I think you'd better be on your way," Emmeline said.

"You won't help me?"

"No. I won't."

Nigel pulled himself straight and put his hat back on. He took an envelope from his overall pockets. "Catherine," he said coldly, "my mother asked me to give this to you before she left. She likes to give a little something to the servants."

I swear he said that word "servants" with extra poison in his voice. I didn't want to take the envelope, but he pushed it into my hands. "Catherine" was written on it in shaky, spidery letters. Inside, something slid as I tipped the envelope. A coin for a *servant.* I sighed and slipped the envelope into my pocket, and Nigel hurried off, his idiotic overalls flapping around his legs.

Just then, Knee-High hurried up. "Was that man b-b-bothering you?" he panted.

"No, he wasn't bothering us," Emmeline said. She dimpled. "I mean, he used to bother *me,* tremendously. But he doesn't any more. It isn't possible for anyone to bother me less, in fact."

Knee-High stared at her, a slow understanding spreading across his face like the sun coming up.

Emmeline looked into his eyes so happily, so sweetly, that it made me feel strange, hot and cold and prickly all over.

Knee-High smiled. I thought he looked handsome, even with his face all dirty. He held out his big hand to my sister, and this time she took it. I felt my eyes fill up as the two of them started down the street. I was so happy. But I felt a pang of loneliness too.

Emmeline stopped after a few steps. "Come on, Cabby!" she called, and I ran to catch up.

A short time later, Ma and Emmeline and I headed for home, Ma urging Lightning and Bolt out of their usual slow plod. It was late, and Orin and Jesse were home alone. All three of us sat squished together on the wagon seat, partly to keep warm. There was a chill in the air that said September wasn't far away, and the wind swirled in strange circles. We saw lightning in the distance, flickering between the sky and the ground. "I hope that means rain, not more fires," Ma said anxiously.

Seemed like there was always something more to worry about. I guess we didn't have to worry about false claims against our land, now that Mr. Mortimer—Mr. J. B. Wentworth, rather—had run off. Nigel Ashford's land-grabbing scheme would fall apart without a land agent he could bribe. But we had plenty of other worries, and the biggest one was money.

I shivered and snuggled closer to Emmeline. It was still summer, the dry prairie grasses still rustled all around us. But I almost thought I saw snowflakes swirling in the dusk. Winter wasn't all that far away.

Chapter 40

The next two weeks were hard. I checked the corn every day, but there was nothing I could do about the wilting, browning leaves. Each day without moisture meant smaller kernels on the ears. Ma and I tried to break more sod in the north field, but we couldn't manage the plow. So every day we watched the corn, watched the well, watched the lightning—and watched the mail for a letter from Pa.

The Nybergs came by one afternoon. They hadn't gotten any money from Nigel, but they were leaving anyway, after they harvested what they could. "Iss just too much, too hard," Mr. Nyberg said. Mrs. Nyberg cried, and so did Emmeline. I did too, to tell the truth. Ma fixed the children some cornbread. I went to bed that night feeling scared. The wind was gusting, and I heard a distant sound that might have been thunder, but I didn't dare pin my hopes on rain.

The next morning, though, a wonderful sound pulled me out of sleep. *Hush-hush, plink, plink, plink.* I stumbled out of bed and pushed through the curtain wall. Rain— actual rain—was streaming past the windows, falling on the sod roof, and plinking into a basin on the floor.

"Ma, it's raining!" I said.

Ma turned from the stove. "Yes, it is, Cabby." Her face shone with happiness.

"What time is it?" I said. It felt late, even though the house was dark. "I'm sorry . . . I'll go milk Lissie now."

"Never mind, sleepy-head," said a deep, laughing voice. "It's done."

"Pa!" I flew to him, and he wrapped me in a big, damp hug. Orin stood by the stove with a shovelful of buffalo chips, beaming. Emmeline leaned against a bureau, gazing at Pa with shining eyes. Jesse had his arms around Pa's waist. The rain on the roof made our little house seem cozy, like a bear's den.

"When did you get here? And what's happening—" I started to ask, but Ma shushed me.

"Set the table, Cabby, and Pa can tell us all about it over breakfast."

"Oh, chickees, I wish you could have seen Denver," Pa said at breakfast, forking a bite of pancake. A drop of water plopped onto the table, and Ma moved a bowl to catch the drip. "You turn around and, bang, there are the Rocky Mountains! It gave me a start every time. I stayed at the Mammoth Sleeping Palace—five hundred beds, if you can believe it."

"Did you sell a lot of watches?" Orin asked eagerly.

"Ah, well," Pa said, rubbing his hair, "there were . . . impediments."

Ma looked down at her plate.

"What's *pediments*?" Jesse asked.

"In this case, son, it's the narrow-minded attitude of

certain members of our government." Pa glanced at Ma before going on. "Though why they would want to clog the wheels of enterprise, I don't understand."

"What do you mean, Pa?" Emmeline said.

"What I mean is, it turns out you need a license to be a drummer. And folks are most unreasonable if you don't happen to have a hundred dollars to pay for one."

"A hundred dollars!" Orin echoed wonderingly.

"A hundred dollars *a year,*" Pa said. He went on, talking about his adventures in Denver—not money-making ones, it seemed—but I stopped listening. Instead, I watched Ma. I could tell from the slump of her shoulders that she'd heard this kind of thing before. Of course she had: there was Black's Special Tonic, and the sure-bet salt well . . . maybe Aunt Tildy was right when she called them "foolish ventures."

But when Ma lifted her head to look at Pa, her expression wasn't angry. It was full of love.

For sure, true love was a puzzling thing.

After breakfast, all six of us crammed into the doorway of the house, the boys in front of Ma and Pa, Emmeline and me on either side. It was so good to be together again, so good to see the rain falling in sheets across the dry prairie. I thought about our corn plants drinking up the water, their kernels plumping out. I thought about the scorched ground near Mrs. Lewis's stable, and how green shoots would soon poke up.

A flash of lightning seemed to crack the sky open; thunder answered with a *crash-crash-boom*. The rain fell so hard I could barely see the cow shed. Snuff whined and nosed at Ma's hand, and she patted his head reassuringly.

She murmured something to Pa. I heard "money" and "milk cow."

"Sell Ulysses?" Pa said out loud. Then he lowered his voice. I couldn't hear what he said, but it wasn't "no."

I gulped. Part of me had been holding out, waiting to see if Pa's watch-selling would succeed. But I knew the answer now.

I pulled away from Pa's side. "Getting too wet, Cabbage?" he said.

"I guess." I went inside and pulled Mrs. Shaw's letter from under my pillow. It seemed to weigh a hundred pounds. I sat down and read it again, hoping maybe I had misunderstood the words. No, the meaning was the same: all I had to do was knock at the door of Ironwood Manor, and I could start making two dollars a week again, working for the Banisters. Maybe I could ask for two dollars and twenty-five cents, now that I was an experienced housemaid.

"What are you doing?" It was Emmeline, her hair spangled with rain drops. She sat beside me on the bed and looked at what I was holding. "Wait, Cabby. You're not thinking of . . .?"

I nodded, swallowing the big lump in my throat.

She put her arm across my shoulders. "It's too awful to contemplate, you going away again."

"No need to be dramatic," I said, trying to sound as sensible as Ma. But tears slid down my cheeks.

"I'm serious, Cabby. There's got to be another way. Didn't Lady Ashford send you some money?"

"Oh, yeah. But unless it's a lump of gold, a coin isn't going to help us much."

"You mean you didn't open her letter?" Emmeline said. "Where is it?"

I got up without enthusiasm and found the letter still in the pocket of my smoky-smelling dress from the day of the fire. I opened the envelope, but what slid out wasn't a coin. It was my brooch! I must have lost it in Lady Ashford's bedroom one of the few times I went in there. How strange to think of her tucking it into an envelope.

I went to the mirror and fastened the brooch carefully to my collar, smiling at my reflection. The blue glass stone glinted dully in the dim light, but I thought it looked beautiful. I had my pa back *and* my brooch back.

Thank you, Milady—this was better than a coin.

"Cabby," Emmeline said, interrupting my thoughts. "Was there anything else? A letter?"

I sat on the bed and pulled a thick, creamy piece of writing paper from the envelope. For some reason, I was reluctant to read the letter. I didn't know for sure that Lady Ashford was dead, but this still felt like a message from beyond the grave. I handed the paper to my sister, and she read the words out loud.

Dear Catherine,

When I said I was in your debt, I was not referring to monetary obligation. Nevertheless, you may think of this as a repayment for your kindness. I trust it will help your family.

I arrived in this country with a low opinion of Americans, but I leave it with a higher one.

Sincerely,

Lady Beatrice Carlotta Ann Ashford

Emmeline dropped the letter to her lap. "Cabby," she said slowly, "what else is in the envelope?"

My hands shaking, I opened the envelope again and pulled out one ten-dollar and two twenty-dollar bank notes. I laid them on the bed. It was more money than I'd ever seen in one place. As the rain drummed on the roof, I just stared at the notes.

"I . . . I can't believe she did this." Mrs. Shaw was right about Lady Ashford, I supposed, about her kindness. I had misjudged her, just as she had misjudged me at first.

Ma pushed the curtain aside and stepped into our little bedroom. "What are you . . .? My goodness!"

Pa came in behind her and stopped short, speechless.

"It's from Lady Ashford," Emmeline said. "Can you believe it?"

"I never asked for money, Ma," I said quickly. "It's a gift."

"Today is a day of gifts," Ma whispered.

"Ma, Pa, say it's enough!" Emmeline cried. "Say that Cabby doesn't have to be a housemaid again."

"A housemaid again?" Ma said. "What are you talking about?"

I stood up and handed Ma the letter about the job at the Banisters'. She read it then looked at me long and hard. There was something in her expression I had never seen before: not just love but . . . admiration, maybe. "You would do this, Cabby?"

When I nodded, she nodded back with tears brimming in her eyes. For Ma, this was like the warmest hug.

"Fifty dollars is six months' pay," Pa said when he'd read the letter. "I reckon Cabby doesn't have to go work for any Lady anywhere, not for now, anyway."

Ma pulled a handkerchief from her sleeve and blew her nose. "I reckon not." And that was that.

My heart and mind too full for words, I threw a shawl over my head and slipped outside. The rain still fell, but lightly. Ragged clouds chased each other across the gray sky, patches of blue opening up here and there. I climbed onto the wall of the well and looked out over the shed, the chicken coop with Ma's biddies huddled inside, the corn field with its tall, strong stalks, and the acres of grassland beyond.

Distant thunder rumbled as the storm moved off across the prairie. It wasn't hard to imagine that the sound was the rumble of hooves, that a herd of buffalo swept across the grasslands. It was sad to think the big beasts were gone. And the tribes who depended on the buffalo—not gone, but pushed out, forced to live in a strange place and in a strange way.

I won't forget, I vowed to Eli. I *won't forget who this land used to belong to.*

In the meantime, I was glad that this particular square of prairie would *not* belong to the son of an English Earl. Starting tomorrow, if it didn't rain again, I would get out there with Pa, work on breaking sod in the north field, maybe in time for a fall planting. Our field, our land.

The Potts family was still pinched, money-wise. But I felt as rich as a queen. Or a duchess, as Pa had called me.

Cabby Potts, Duchess of Dirt. As titles went, it wasn't a bad one.

Chapter 41

A few weeks later, we hired help and harvested the corn crop. Like I was hoping, Pa planted the corn field in winter wheat when the harvest was done. But he didn't get too far in breaking the north field before winter slammed into Kansas like a runaway train. It seemed like one blizzard would end and another one would roar across the prairie. I just about went crazy cooped up inside. Even with the money from Lady Ashford, Ma was unhappy about spending so much on coal and hay and supplies. Pa got a real, money-making job shoveling snow for the railroads, but it was dangerous work, and we were all nervous until he came home.

I hoped he was home for good, but I couldn't be sure. Pa loved us, I knew, but part of him was restless. That's just the way he was.

Finally, at the end of February, there was a real thaw. The snow melted down to dirty piles, and wide stretches of prairie opened to the soft air. Winter wasn't over, but we felt like spring was just about here. Knee-High visited when he could, and he and Emmeline would walk outside, coming back wind-blown and happy. She went to town a lot too, and when she wasn't working in the post office, she helped Knee-High organize his store. All the customers said that things were easier to find. The two of them weren't engaged yet—Emmeline decided she was too young—but it was going to happen. Even Moonbeam, Knee-High's cat, was learning to like my sister, or at least tolerate her.

I was in town one morning when I spotted a notice on the wall of the bank:

Public Auction

Fine Household Goods, Farming Implements and Choice
Livestock
Saturday, March 6
Ashford Manor, Prince Albert, Kansas

I was puzzling over the notice—why would Nigel have an auction?— when Mr. and Mrs. Shaw bustled up. "Cabby!" Mrs. Shaw cried. "It does me good to see you after such a long winter!"

I hugged both of them. "Did you put this up?" I asked.

"Yes, we did," Mr. Shaw said. "'Aven't you 'eard? Ashford Manor's to be sold."

"What?"

"It's true. The Master's already gone back to England," Mrs. Shaw said.

Mr. Shaw shook his head. "'E got 'imself into debt, if the truth be known, wot with 'is wagering, and 'is spending ways. Now 'e's going to try 'is hand at lawyering, or some such occupation."

I shook my head too. What had I been thinking, trying

to marry Emmeline off to someone like Nigel? But part of me felt mighty satisfied. *We* were going to make it here, and Nigel Ashford was not, just like Knee-High had predicted way back when.

"What about . . . ?" I was going to say "Eli" but stopped myself, blushing. "What about you? Are you going to England?"

Mrs. Shaw beamed like she had just won a spelling bee. "That we are *not,* lass! We 'ave just purchased . . . show 'er, Mr. Shaw."

Mr. Shaw pulled a paper from his pocket. I skimmed from line to line: *Bill of Sale . . . Prouty Boarding House . . . Herbert and Mary Shaw . . .*

"We've 'ad enough of being servants," Mrs. Shaw said, and I hugged her again, a big smile spreading across my face. "Wot with so many people coming west," she went on, "we believe the time is ripe for a new boarding house. What do you think we should call it?"

"'Ow about the Mary Shaw?" Mr. Shaw said, looking fondly at his wife.

Mrs. Shaw giggled, if you can believe it. "Nonsense! Now, Cabby, we might 'ire you to clean from time to time."

"I'll think about it," I said. And I meant it.

The auction at Ashford Manor attracted quite a crowd. Everybody from Slocum City and beyond wanted a chance to stroll through the house and barns, fingering all the fine things. I wandered with the crowd, although it made me feel strange, and a little sad. But I had to laugh when a farmer picked up Nigel's chamber pot. "Ain't this a fancy bowl—my Molly would love it for her soup."

When the bidding on household goods started, Mrs. Buchanan bought some towels for the hotel, Mrs. Wattles bought a nice sewing basket for fifty cents, and Mrs. Snopes bought a single linen napkin for three cents. "Mr. Lordy-pants never did fix my window," she sniffed. "Good riddance to him!" Bridget O'Donovan bought a set of plain white plates—I didn't tell her those were the ones the "servants" ate off. She and Bub were planning a wedding as soon as he finished their wood frame house.

Nobody bid on the fine china or the silver or most of the furniture, although Knee-High did buy a fancy needlework chair after Emmeline mentioned how refined it was. It was basically useless, if you asked me.

The bidding on the farm goods was more serious, and people spent precious dollars on pitchforks, hoes, and rakes. Bub Skyler bought some nails and bolts and such. Pa bought a sharp scythe, and Ma said she liked that better than the gewgaws he had wanted to bid on.

The horses were the main attraction. A homesteader from way out on the prairie bought Nigel's two plow horses with the feathers on their legs. "William and Robert?" I heard him say. "Naw, they'll be Billy and Bob at my place."

I was sad when the bidding on Three-Legs began. We couldn't afford him, but I hated to see him go. I felt better when Mr. Rouse won the bid, even though he said he was thinking about going back to Texas, where he was from.

As the bidding on the other horses went on, I slipped into the stable, hoping to find a certain *Kehimi*. Yes, there he was, straightening out a pile of bridles, tethers, and harnesses.

"Hey, you," Eli said.

"Hey, yourself." I couldn't think what to say next, so I fiddled with a rope from the pile, listening to the hum of the auctioneer's voice, "Fifty dollars, fifty dollars, who'll give me sixty dollars . . .?"

"Listen, Cabby," Eli said suddenly. "Ma found an envelope under her door the other day."

I looked hard at the weaving in the rope. "You don't say."

"There was five dollars inside, and no signature. You know anything about that?"

I hung the rope on a hook, careful not to look at him. The gift had been my idea, with Ma and Pa in agreement. "Not a thing," I said. "Guess it's just her good fortune." I smiled to myself, thinking about the reverse arithmetic of gifts. Seemed like giving made people richer instead of poorer.

"She saw a scrawny girl running off from her place that very day," Eli said. "Guess it was a coincidence."

"Yup, guess so."

"Well, Ma says thank you—to fortune, if that's what you want to call it," Eli said. He picked up a pair of snarled reins, frowning over the knots.

"Give me those, clumsy." I took the reins and undid the knots. "What are you going to do now?" I asked. "About a job, I mean." I held my breath, hoping he wasn't going to Ironwood Manor or some other Prince Albert place.

"Just work at my ma's stable. Things are picking up a bit. Maybe offer to do some herding for folks too. There are laws now—people can't let their cattle go free."

I looked down to hide my grin. "Guess I'll be seeing more of you, then."

"Guess so."

There was a silence. When I lifted my head, Eli looked at me with that sly sideways smile. "You know what? I'd kiss you if you weren't so ornery."

What?

"I'd kiss *you* if you weren't so ugly," I said. It was all I could think of.

"I'd like to see you try!"

That was a challenge if I ever heard one. I leaned over and planted my very first girl-boy kiss on Eli's cheek. It happened so fast I didn't know what to do afterwards. So I just scooted out of the barn. I wasn't sure which I liked better, kissing Eli or fighting with him.

The good news was, the Potts family was staying right here in Kansas. With any luck, I'd have plenty of time to figure it out.

The End

Author's Note

I f you drive across Kansas today, you'll see cities, towns, farms, and trees. But in the early 1800's, much of Kansas was flat, treeless prairie. I'm fascinated by the prairie and by the early settlers who transformed the land. I've read piles of books and journals about Kansas history, enjoying the first-hand accounts I found in the dusty shelves of Rutgers University libraries. Most of these books take the 1850s as their starting place. At that time, before my story begins, Kansas was ground zero in the bloody battle between pro-slavery and free-state (anti-slavery) militants. Eventually, Kansas entered the Union as a free state.

But of course the history of Kansas goes back long before white settlers arrived.

The Kiowa Tribe

The Kiowa were one of several tribes of Native Americans who lived on the Great Plains for thousands of years before Euro-Americans arrived. (I use the term "Indian" in my story, since it was used at the time, but "Native American" or "Native" is more accurate and is preferred by the Kiowa tribe.) The Kiowa were a nomadic tribe, meaning that they moved from place to place, following the migration of the buffalo. Traditionally, they were a warrior society, with young boys beginning as *Polanyup* (rabbits) and progressing in rank as they learned new skills in hunting and fighting. Kiowa life revolved around the buffalo; even the tipis they lived in were made from buffalo hides. Buffalo hunts, as Eli tells Cabby, were exciting chases across the prairie.

The Kiowa way of life, and that of other Native Americans of the Great Plains, was almost destroyed by the arrival of white settlers. The white people brought diseases like smallpox and cholera (the "sickness that got into the water," as Eli calls it). Settlers also built farms and ranches that disrupted buffalo migration and feeding areas, sometimes in areas officially designated for Native people. Buffalo were slaughtered by the thousands, for their hides but also just for sport. As Eli points out, the American government did nothing to stop the destruction; in fact, President Ulysses S. Grant considered the killing of the buffalo to be a solution to the "Indian Problem." By 1850, the Kiowa were forced to hunt antelope and jackrabbits, and by 1870 the buffalo were nearly extinct.

Starved of food and land, the Kiowa had no choice but to sign the Medicine Lodge Treaty in 1867, agreeing to move to Indian Territory reservations in present-day Oklahoma. The Kiowa people were required to farm instead of hunt, part of a policy called forced assimilation. Kiowa and other Native children were forced to attend government schools that suppressed their language, dress, and culture.

In spite of the odds against them, the Kiowa people survived, and many still live in Oklahoma. Today, they are reviving their culture and maintaining a strong community.

Homesteading on the Prairie

"Go West, young man," is a saying attributed to New York newspaperman Horace Greeley. In 1862, the government passed the Homestead Act, which opened large areas of previously Native American land to settlers. Most homesteaders were people from Eastern or Midwestern states looking for better opportunities; some also emigrated from Sweden, England, Russia, or Germany. Homesteaders could claim a quarter-mile square section, then live on it for five years. After planting crops and building a dwelling, the homesteaders could "prove up," and for eighteen dollars total, the land would be theirs. And Cabby is right—women could stake claims of their own, but only if they were not married.

Although homesteading might seem like "a deal at twice the price," as Pa says, many of our current beliefs about pioneer life are romanticized. Half of all homesteaders were never able to prove up on their claims. Part of this failure was because of incredibly difficult conditions. In Kansas, grasshoppers ate their way across the state in 1874, covering every inch of land and destroying all the crops. There were also fires, harsh winters, and drought, not to mention the lack of trees that led people to build houses out of squares of prairie sod. No wonder the state motto of Kansas is *Ad Astra per Aspera:* "to the stars through difficulty."

But another reason homesteaders failed was because the "deal" wasn't as good as it seemed. The best land was often owned by the railroads and wasn't available to homesteaders. People called speculators grabbed up huge stretches of desirable land and sold the land for a profit. They found ways of getting around homesteading rules, like hiring people to file dummy claims or moving "dwellings" on wheels from claim to claim. Mr. J. B. Wentworth is fictional, but there certainly were crooked land agents. Ordinary homesteaders started off with very little—and sometimes ended up with nothing. Still, approximately ten percent of land in the United States was claimed and settled by homesteaders.

A Settlement of British Aristocrats

I was surprised to learn that British people, beginning in the early 1800s, were fascinated by the American West; they eagerly read novels and travelers' tales of wilderness adventures. Wealthy aristocrats even crossed the Atlantic for hunting trips on the prairies, complete with personal servants and brass beds for their tents. Nigel Ashford is fictional, but I imagined that his father might have made such a trip and shot the buffalo on his study wall. Some of these aristocrats also began to see the potential to increase their fortunes in America.

Prince Albert is based on an actual settlement of British aristocrats on the windswept, short-grass region of central Kansas. In 1872, a London silk merchant named Sir George Grant bought 50,000 acres near the Kansas Pacific railroad, naming his settlement "Victoria." He enticed wealthy English families with newspaper ads describing "green prairies, rolling like gentle swells in the ocean, starred and gemmed with flowers." More than 200 English settlers arrived, bringing their thoroughbred horses and fine furniture. They enjoyed a life of games, hunts (with jackrabbits and coyotes instead of foxes), fancy balls, and dinner parties—the refinement of English high society transplanted to the prairie.

Many of the English settlers were second sons, or, in Nigel's case, fifth sons. Because of rules of primogeniture, only the oldest son could inherit a family estate. So, cheap land in America seemed like a good solution to the "swarming manhood" problem among land-owning families. Unfortunately, these privileged young men knew little about farming, and they found Kansas life difficult. One of them wrote home complaining of the terrible heat and "regular gales." He requested an even bigger allowance (or "remittance") from his father. Ultimately, the English settlers of Victoria couldn't make farming work. By 1879, Victoria was abandoned, to be taken over by Russian immigrants with less money but more perseverance.

I was intrigued by the contrast between homesteaders in their makeshift houses and aristocrats in their limestone mansions, living just miles from each other. It's tempting to think that the hard-working homesteaders were more decent and egalitarian (unbiased) than their class-conscious English neighbors. However, as Cabby comes to realize, Americans had—and still have—their own prejudices.

In Cabby Potts, I tried to portray a girl growing into more awareness of her world, with all its imperfections.

She learns to use her voice to make that world a better place, something I hope we all can do.

Acknowledgements

I'm grateful for the resources of the Kansas Historical Society for general Kansas history and for information about the Kiowa tribe. I'm also grateful for videos put out by elders in the Kiowa community (kiowatribe.org). They helped me learn a few Kiowa words and are doing their part to preserve the Kiowa language. Other experts made thoughtful suggestions on Native representation in my manuscript.

To learn about homesteading, I consulted primary sources (journals and memoirs) as well as several excellent books. Some of them are: *The American West: A New Interpretive History,* by Robert Hine and John Mack Faragher; *A Shovel of Stars: the Making of the American West 1800 to the Present,* by Ted Morgan; and *Pioneer Women: Voices from the Kansas Frontier,* by Joanna Stratton. I especially loved *Pioneer Women,* beginning with the cover image of a gaunt-faced woman pushing a wheelbarrow full of buffalo chips.

I am indebted to Peter Pagnamenta's book *Prairie Fever: British Aristocrats in the American West 1830–1890* for information about the Victoria Colony and British fascination with the American frontier in general. All my quotes about the British in America are from *Prairie Fever.*

Of course, I'm particularly grateful to Michele McAvoy of Little Press Publishing for seeing the potential in *Cabby Potts, Duchess of Dirt.* I'm grateful to my husband,

Paul Wilford, for his patience and encouragement. And I couldn't have written this without the help of my talented, professional critique group: Shauna Cagan, Brian Gonsar, Naomi Gruer, Theresa Julian, and Marilyn Ostermiller. Without their unflagging dedication and willingness to read draft after draft, this book would not have happened. Thank you!

About the Author

Kathleen Wilford was born in Panama and has lived in four different countries and three different states—but never in Kansas. She studied literature at Cornell University and at Rutgers University in New Jersey, where she now teaches writing. When she's not teaching or writing, Kathleen can be found outdoors, chasing her disobedient dog.

Cabby Potts, Duchess of Dirt is Kathleen's debut novel for kids.

Connect with Kathleen at kathleenwilford.com